"Tell me something, do you love me?"

"Yes, but—" Anona's breath was a gasp as she answered him. She had confessed to a love for him that she had not even been conscious of feeling. Yet it was true, now that she allowed herself to admit the fact.

Shane's eyes were lit with a taunting triumph at having so easily forced the confession from her. "No buts, my love. You're mine. You're marrying me."

There was a song in her head that deafened her with its sweetness. "Nothing—nothing will stop me," she whispered, resting her hands against his chest.

"Not even your father?"

She sobered. "I don't know." Her voice was suddenly uncertain. She did love Shane, as deeply as she loved her father. But how would it ever work out…?

Other titles by

LILIAN PEAKE
IN HARLEQUIN PRESENTS

Other titles by

LILIAN PEAKE
IN HARLEQUIN ROMANCES

Many of these titles, and other titles in the Harlequin Romance series, are available at your local bookseller. For a free catalogue listing all available Harlequin Presents and Harlequin Romances, send your name and address to:

HARLEQUIN READER SERVICE,
M.P.O. Box 707,
Niagara Falls, N.Y. 14302

Canadian address:
Stratford, Ontario, Canada N5A 6W2

LILIAN PEAKE

dangerous deception

Harlequin Books

TORONTO·LONDON·NEW YORK·AMSTERDAM
SYDNEY·HAMBURG·PARIS·STOCKHOLM

Harlequin Presents edition published April 1980
ISBN 0-373-10353-0

Original hardcover edition published in 1979
by Mills & Boon Limited

CHAPTER ONE

FOR some time the monster truck had been following Anona closely, but try as she might, she had not been able to understand why. Her eyes had sought the driving mirror, but all she had been able to see was the scarlet paint of the vehicle behind her. The windscreen had towered so far above the top of her car it had been impossible to see it, let alone see through it. Her window was wound down to its lowest point, letting the cooling breeze circulate. It had lifted the strands of her fair hair, fanning her neck and giving some relief from the heat of the warm summer day.

The driver must have decided at last to give up the chase and pulled out into the fast lane of the motorway. As the truck came level with her, Anona's head turned to discover the cause of her irritation, for nothing annoyed her more than a giant of the road sticking to her tail like an animal of the wilds running its prey to earth. She frowned across the distance and met the sardonic grin of the man who for so many miles had been her tormentor.

Her instinct was to swear violently at him, hoping he could lip-read. When she did mouth a word or two, all that came was a relatively mild, 'Damn you!' He seemed to guess what she had said because, for a few fleeting seconds, his head had been thrown back in laughter. He had driven on and Anona had lost him.

The memory of his audacity, not to mention the formidable strength inherent in the man's arms, the breadth of his back and the deep tan of his body, exposed as it had been to the waist, lingered on in her mind.

With a sigh of relief Anona realised that she would never see the man again. He was driving an empty truck and it was well-known that all truck drivers without loads drove at a much faster speed in order to get back to their depot and pick up another load as quickly as possible thus earning an extra bonus and adding to their income.

It was as she approached a service station containing a complex of restaurant, small motel, shops and filling station that she became aware of the dryness of her mouth and the inadequacy of the sandwich meal she had eaten a few hours before at around midday.

Lining up the car neatly in a parking place, she got out and locked the doors. As she looked from one building to the other, she noticed a sign indicating the existence at the rear of the complex of a parking area for larger motor vehicles and coaches. It flashed through her mind that the driver of the red monster which had followed her for so many miles might have decided to take a rest and a meal at that particular service station.

The thought had her hesitating, but as her eyes scanned all that the place had to offer she decided that, even if he had, as a truck driver he would have chosen the smaller café rather than the restaurant which she contemplated patronising.

The restaurant was more expensive-looking than she had assumed. It was waitress service, whereas the café had been self-service. There were soft lights and elegant drapes and small pot plants, all of which no doubt added to the cost of the meal. Anona chose a central seat at an empty table for two. When she started to read the menu and saw the prices of the dishes, she almost slid out of her seat and made for the door.

The income on which she and her father lived was meagre and she could afford to order no more than a pot of tea, a scone and jam and maybe a small cake. The order was taken by an attractive waitress with a neat white apron and low-cut black dress. The girl scribbled on a pad, tore off the top copy and placed it on the table, then raised her eyes and smiled over Anona's head.

When she had gone, Anona looked around, attempting to discover the recipient of that smile. It must, she decided, have been male, since such an invitation as it had held could only have been directed towards a member of the opposite sex.

The person who had caught that smile was undoubtedly masculine—Anona had discovered that for herself on her drive along the motorway. Under the shirt and tie which, to her surprise, he now wore, she knew that there was a set of rippling muscles and a broad brown back.

That very male person, whose hair was black and whose features, seen at close quarters, were regular and well-shaped and added up to a decidedly handsome face, plainly enjoyed the game of motorway flirtation which was not at all unknown and which, she had been informed, often reached finality in very intimate circumstances!

In front of the man was a dish which seemed to have been selected from the most expensive section on the menu. Beside his plate stood a glass of no doubt fine vintage wine. He sat there, knife and fork poised. On his face was a smile—the same kind of smile which had been directed at the waitress? Anona doubted it. The smile he had exchanged with that attractive young woman must have held an answer to her invitation. The smile which he turned on to Anona was arrogant and mocking.

Making her expression as reproving as she could, she swung her head away, feeling her shoulder-length fair hair lift and fall. Her order came and moments after setting it down, the waitress moved between the tables to stand at the driver's side. Anona concentrated on pouring out her tea and buttering her scone, refusing to allow her head to turn towards them.

After one bite of her jam-covered scone, however, her head swivelled like a clockwork toy and she studied the two of them. It was plain that they knew each other but how well, Anona would not allow herself to consider. Truck drivers, she told herself, drove long distances. They needed refreshment and rest. Wasn't it also well-known that they needed other things?

There was laughter and the dark-haired waitress leant forward to brush something from the jacket—part of a suit, it seemed—which the man wore over his shirt. 'Dust,' she heard him say. 'Dirty job, truck driving . . .'

Two customers entered and sat at a table. The girl gave the man another warm smile, which he wholeheartedly returned, and went to serve the new arrivals. Again the man looked across at Anona and it was only then that she realised how much she was staring. The blush rose too quickly for her to suppress it, and the man's eyes grew sardonic. Now what was he thinking, Anona wondered— as if she didn't know!

It seemed he skipped the second course and went straight on to coffee. Good, Anona thought, soon he'll go. But he showed no signs of being in a hurry, which was strange for a driver with an empty truck. Something about the man puzzled her. His voice? But she had hardly heard him talk. His neat appearance in the restaurant, after his stripped-to-the-waist act in the cab of the truck? His expensive tastes, his arrogance? The man was an enigma, one she had no intention of even trying to solve. She brushed her mouth with a paper napkin and pushed back her chair.

It was as she reached the door of the restaurant that a hand tapped her shoulder and she swung round to find the truck driver handing her a piece of paper. She had heard a voice calling, but she had been so obsessed with getting away from those mocking eyes, which had not shifted from her all the time the owner of them had slowly drunk his coffee, that she had forgotten the bill!

Colouring deeply, confused and angry, with both herself and the man who had seen it all happen, she muttered a hoarse-voiced 'Thank you' and snatched the piece of paper from him. It's your fault, she wanted to say, for staring at me so rudely. Returning to the interior of the restaurant, she made her way to the cash desk and settled the account.

The woman who dealt with the matter had not even noticed, she was so busy coping with her job. It was left for Anona to explain her error to the man who now stood behind her, waiting to settle his own bill.

'I—I forgot,' she said, folding the receipt into four and then eight. 'I've—I've never done such a thing before.'

The man, with a smile and uplifted eyebrow, nodded as if to say, I've heard that one before. Furious with him, yet knowing she should be grateful, she swung away and this time made it to the open air and her car. She reversed and turned the car to face the road, seeing out of the corner of her eye the man tucking away his change and making for the shops.

Again the open road was before her and a strange sense of freedom—from what, she wondered—sang in her head. She would never see the man again! That was the reason for her pleasure. She put her foot hard on the accelerator and the car sped northwards to Derbyshire and home.

It was some miles on that she noticed a strange noise coming from the car. Since it was not continuous but intermittent, she tried to ignore it.

The car was six years old and she had known for some time that she should have replaced it with a newer model, but the money simply was not available. As her journey progressed, she could not prevent her eyes from straying now and then to search in the driving mirror and the wing mirror for a bright red truck.

No such truck nosed its way forward to drive behind her and she could not suppress a flash of disappointment from zigzagging through her body. At once she chided herself, Why should I be upset if I never see that arrogant creature again? It was obvious how he regarded women—as a means to an end. It did not take much intelligence to know what that 'end' was.

Nor did she doubt the man's ability to 'pull' all the women he wanted. As if his looks weren't enough, she thought, he had to possess a physique and a personality which would surely stir the most undersexed female to life!

The car juddered beneath her, almost petrifying her with fear. Something terrible was happening and she doubted whether she would be able control the car much longer. Before it came to a complete stop, she had the presence of mind to turn the steering wheel and guide the car on to the relative safety of the hard shoulder.

Braking sharply, she sat, head bowed, fighting panic, her hands still gripping the steering wheel. The heat of the sun beat through the open window, and with no breeze created by the car's movement to cool it down, it began to burn her cheek and her exposed shoulder and arm.

Deciding that she could not sit there helplessly in the ridiculous hope that the engine would start again of its own accord, she operated the bonnet lock, got out and walked to the front of the car. Peering into the engine, she was overcome by a terrible feeling of inadequacy. Never had she regretted so much her ignorance of how a car worked.

Even the instruction book which she found in a pocket inside the door was meaningless to her. She stood with it in her hand, gazing from the engine to the diagrams, trying in vain to line the drawings up with the real thing. She knew that even if she managed to do so, there was absolutely nothing she could do to remedy the situation, however simple the repair might prove to be.

Throwing the book on to the rear seat, she stood beside the car, the bonnet lid still open, watching the cars and vans and commercial vehicles speed heedlessly by. When a car did slow down and stop, having pulled in beside her own car, her heart began to beat hard with hope.

'Having trouble?' the man asked, his eyes all over her. Nevertheless she had to admit the truth. 'Oh dear,' he said, 'I know how you feel. What a pity I'm as useless about the practical side of motoring as you are.'

He eyed her again, looking uninhibitedly at her attractions which were accentuated by her sleeveless top and dusty denim slacks. She began to feel uncomfortable. Men! she thought. What does he think I'm doing? Pretending my car's broken down just for fun—the sort of fun *he* has in mind?

'Can I take you on a bit for a drink, then bring you back?' Yes, there it was, that certain look.

She shook her head, mumbling, 'Thanks for stopping.' With relief, she watched him drive on.

It was an unpleasant feeling being parked on the hard shoulder, as though somehow she was committing a crime. It was, of course, the correct place to be parked when one's car had broken down. All the same, the unceasing roar of traffic passing by made Anona long to become part of it again, speeding along to her father and her home. Soon no doubt her father would start worrying, since she could not possibly hope to make up the time that was being lost just standing there helplessly.

There was in the distance, towering high above the other traffic, a scarlet-painted truck. Yes, here it comes, she thought, a monster of the road being driven by the arrogant truck driver with the sardonic smile. Her heart started to beat strangely hard, her eyes fixing themselves on the approaching patch of bright red as if willing it to come to her aid.

What if it didn't? What if the driver missed her despondent figure? What if he saw her, then looked the other way? Beneath that derisive smile of his there was a certain solid dependability. There had to be, hadn't there? she argued desperately. It was surely a quality which most of his kind possessed, transporting as they did consignments of sometimes dangerous fluids, vital supplies of machinery or metals, from one part of the country, one side of the world, to the other?

He was much nearer now. Would he pass or would he stop? Was it her imagination or was he slowing down? He had seen her, he *was* slowing down. Skilfully he man-oeuvred the red giant from the slow lane on to the hard shoulder. There was a sigh as the brakes were applied and the engine sound dropped away to nothing.

The first thing she noticed as he climbed down back-wards from the driving cab was that he had changed out of his suit and was back to ancient jeans, topped by nothing—if that was how his sunburnt body could be described.

He strolled towards her, eyeing with undoubted appre-ciation everything the man in the car had appreciated. There was about this man, however, a touch of insolence. Was it in the boldness of his gaze, the mockery lurking about his lips, the way he hooked his thumbs in his belt? Whatever it was, it struck a chord of fear in Anona's tensing body.

'So we meet again, lady.' The timbre of his voice had her staring. It had about it hallowed places of learning—Oxbridge?—of culture and intelligence. She knew about such things, since her father had, before misfortune had struck him, been a university professor. 'Has the superior young lady with her nose in the air—and who, tut, tut, omitted to settle her bill until reminded—come to grief?'

She eyed him warily. If he had been a straightforward, down-to-earth truck driver, she would have known how to deal with his impudence. But nothing about this man quite added up.

She answered evenly, 'I'm not superior, I'm just an ordinary girl. My nose is where it should be—straight in front of my face, and it's not a habit of mine to walk out without paying. And,' a real driver would take this on the chin, 'my greatest grief was having you, of all those drivers,' she nodded towards the motorway, 'come to my aid.'

He enjoyed the joke, just as he had when she had sworn mildly at him way back when he had finally overtaken her. So he had taken it on the chin. Did that make him the genuine article?

He continued to study her, folding his arms. Why, she wondered, did he not ask, What's the trouble? 'I've broken down,' she said, hoping the statement would lead to action on his part.

'You have?' He pretended to frown. 'You look completely mobile, not to mention nubile, to me.'

She flushed. 'What erudite words,' she snapped, 'for a truck driver!' He smiled but did not speak. She nodded towards the monster which towered over her car. 'Have you come far with that?'

'From Tilbury Docks.'

'Delivering a load?'

'Chemicals. For export.'

'Have you been a truck driver long?'

His smile was derisive, as if he knew she was delving. 'Since I graduated from driving toy cars into the garden walls. I was born with a steering wheel in my hands. I cut my teeth on spanners and was fed with a diet of nuts and bolts.'

Anona forced a loud sigh. This was getting nowhere. 'My father will be worrying if I don't do something soon.' She swallowed her pride. 'Please will you help me?'

He did not change his position. His eyes hardened a little and he looked her over again as if it was his turn to size her up and place her on the social scale, except that his survey was carried out silently. Unlike the girl he was scrutinising, he appeared to come to a conclusion. Whether or not it was correct Anona was soon to learn.

'The instruction book is on the back seat,' she said, going towards the car. He did not move. 'Will you——' she pushed back a straying hair, 'will you come ... ?'

She got into the back of the car, picked up the book and moved across, leaving room for him. Slowly he approached, bent his head and got in beside her. Nervously she flicked through the book, the diagrams dancing in front of her.

His proximity, with his upper half devoid of clothing, was overpowering.

Wondering when he would ask her about the events leading up to the car's breakdown, she slanted a glance at him. The way he was looking at her jolted her heart. In his eyes was the same look as had been present in the other man's. That man had driven on. This one had stopped. If *that* was in his mind, then he could go to—— She knew that without his help, she might be stranded there for hours.

Her large blue eyes turned up to his, her oval-shaped face creased into an appealing smile. 'Please, Mr—I don't know your name.'

'Call me Shane.'

'Shane, would you look at my car? It's——'

'Is it? There's nothing wrong with it, is there?' She stared at him. 'Okay, little lady, when do we start? It's a bit public here, but——'

Her hand swung before she could stop it. The noise it made as it hit his cheek was like a thunderclap, even over the continuous noise of the traffic.

His hand shot out and caught her wrist. He said, through his teeth, 'Why, you——'

Under the pressure of his fingers, she thought her wrist would snap. Tears crept into her eyes, but she bit her top lip rather than cry out. His eyes blazed. 'You pass the hours and the miles on that motorway,' he gritted, 'playing cat and mouse with me—go away, come closer, overtake me then I'll overtake you, then follow me because I know a nice little hotel where you can make my intimate acquaintance. Then, when you play one of the oldest tricks of all—pretend you've got car trouble—and I respond in the way you've been asking for for hours, you turn all virtuous and innocent——'

Pale now, her heart pounding, she said, speaking each word clearly, 'Get out of my car.'

He threw her a last contemptuous look and did as she

asked. When he slammed her car door and strode towards his truck, she realised that in a few minutes he wouldn't be there any more. He would be a red speck in the distance, while she would still be stranded with a broken-down car.

The engine of the truck roared to life. She flung out of the car and raced to his door. The window was open and she threw back her head and shouted,

'Please, *please*, Shane, it *has* gone wrong.' Her hand waved towards the car. 'It doesn't go, nothing works. It's true ...'

He sat high up in his cab, looking down at her. She could not read his face, but the engine was still running. It could only mean he had taken such offence at the slap on his cheek, he refused to relent. Hopelessly she turned away to gaze once more at the speeding, unheeding cars.

CHAPTER TWO

THE noise of the truck's engine died away. Anona did not dare to glance round in case the sound of a door opening, of feet descending, was imagination.

'Okay,' said a voice behind her. 'I'll take a look. If it really has broken down, maybe I'll apologise.'

She threw him a look of gratitude brilliant enough to make any man glow. This man remained as illuminated as an unlighted candle. As his head bent over the engine and his hand probed here and there, Anona felt a surge of trust in this man called Shane who had come to her rescue. Instinctively she knew, by the way he examined the component parts of the mechanism in front of him, that his knowledge of the workings of a car was sufficient to enable him to carry out any repairs necessary to get her car back on the road.

She was so convinced of this that his next words came as a shock. 'I think it's a major repair job. Tell me exactly what happened.' He listened while she explained, nodding at the end. He pulled a rag from a pocket and wiped his hands, stuffing the rag back afterwards. 'I guess it's the gears that have gone. Short of crawling under the car, I can't confirm my suspicions, but I'm certain my hunch is correct.'

He got into the driving seat, turned the ignition key a number of times and finally had the engine firing. When the gears proved stubborn and, despite his attempts, the car failed to move, he nodded. 'Sorry.' He withdrew the keys and pocketed them, getting out of the car. 'You won't be needing these for a while.'

'What are you going to do with them?'

'Action is needed. You agree?'

16

Anona nodded, her expression expectant. Was he not going to leave her stranded, as she had dreaded?

'There's only one thing to do. You'll have to leave the car here, take out all your belongings and lock it. On our way north, we'll have to find a phone box and ring a garage and arrange to have your car towed to it. Their mechanics can examine it and if possible, repair it.'

'Our', 'we'? Was she going too? 'Where do I come in?' she asked, frowning.

'You "come in" to my cab.'

'You mean you'll give me a lift in your truck?'

'That was my intention. What's wrong? Beneath your dignity?'

'Of course not, but——'

'You don't trust me?' He rubbed the cheek she had slapped. 'Did I remember to apologise?'

'Why? I was the one who did the hitting.'

He shook his head. 'I said I'd say sorry if I found the car was really out of action. Now it's your turn.'

With reluctance she said, 'I'm sorry I slapped your face. But,' she blurted out, 'you deserved it.'

His eyelids lowered a fraction. 'Did I? When attractive young women drivers play games with me, they deserve whatever comes their way.' He looked at his watch. 'Come on, you've wasted enough of my time already. I have to get back to the depot.'

It took only a few minutes to take her suitcases and other items from inside the car and carry them across to the truck. As the man called Shane stowed them away, she asked, 'Will your employer sack you if you're late?'

He smiled slightly. 'He'd throw me right out on my ear.'

As Anona gazed up at the driving cab she drew back instinctively.

'Afraid?' he taunted as he stood, hands on hips, gazing at her.

'It's so big.'

'Come on, I'll give you a lift up.' He stretched his arm

towards the handle—and Anona saw for the first time the name of the company for which the man worked. 'Brodie's' she exclaimed, '*Brodie's!*' She turned to him. 'It would have to be Brodie's you work for.'

He lifted an eyebrow. 'What have Brodie's ever done to you?'

The door was wide open now, but she hesitated. 'I don't think I want a lift in one of *their* vehicles.'

'For pity's sake—what's your name?' She told him. 'Anona, haven't I spent enough time trying to sort out your problems?' Her foot lifted to the lower step and she felt strong hands span her slim waist.

She could not explain the feeling that coursed through her at the man's touch. All she knew at that moment was that she did not want the contact to end. He thought her hesitation was due to her inability to bring her other foot up to rest on the top step. His hands slipped upwards, sliding over her breasts and coming to rest under her armpits.

When at last she found herself sitting in the passenger seat and her body appreciating the almost new upholstery behind her back and beneath her, she sighed. It was all less intimidating than she had thought. In fact, the most daunting object in that driving cab was the driver himself as he climbed into his seat.

'You're a lightweight,' he said, his eyes busy with the dials on the dashboard. 'How come there's no ring on your finger?'

Brightly she answered, as if she hadn't a care in the world, 'Two days ago I ended my engagement.'

He looked at her quickly. 'No regrets?'

'Not one.' And, strangely, she discovered she meant it. Her eyes were everywhere. 'What's that?' She pointed behind and above.

'A bunk bed. Storage cupboards, a place for a change of clothes. It's this year's model. Didn't you guess by the registration number?'

'I didn't even notice.'

'You should cultivate observation. From this height I see a lot. Your car's registration plate, for example. From it I knew your car was six years old. I also guessed from it— since you were heading in that direction—that you live in Derbyshire. Of course, you could have bought the car there and——'

She broke in, 'You're right. My father and I live near Bakewell.'

'Is that so? Then maybe we'll meet again some time.'

'Is—is that where you live?'

'Brodie's depot isn't far from there. By the way, I asked you before—what harm has Brodie's ever done to you?'

'Not me. My father.' A long pause. 'They crippled him for life. He can only get around in a wheelchair.'

The man called Shane checked the driving mirror and pulled out into the fast lane. 'Sorry to hear that,' he said. 'Was it long ago?'

'About eighteen months. We've just sold our house in London. It was old and in need of repair, which is why it took quite a long time finding a buyer. I signed the contract yesterday on my father's behalf.'

'So you've been in London?' For the past week, she told him. 'And you were on your way home when your car broke down? Who's been looking after your father?'

'Our neighbours, Mr and Mrs Patterson.' She looked around the cab, at the fixtures, the large steering wheel, the strong arms and hands that controlled it. A compulsion to touch those hands and arms gripped her and she glanced shyly up at the profile of the man. He had, she thought, more than his fair share of good looks. He must have been conscious of her regard. His head turned quickly and caught her eyes on him. Embarrassment brought a flush to her cheeks and he laughed.

'Age thirty,' he said. 'Unmarried, healthy and virile. Plenty of money in the bank with no one but myself to spend it on. Do I make a bad bargain? I warn you, where women are concerned, I have very little staying power. And I do mean *staying* power. If you're willing to take me on those terms, Anona, I'm yours.'

'Thank you,' she said, clasping her hands, 'but no.' Anger had sprung from nowhere, and she could not think why. 'I've just broken loose from one entanglement, I don't propose to go headlong into another. Not for a long time. And certainly not with a man I couldn't rely on to stay faithful to me. And most definitely,' tossing him a defiant glance, 'I wouldn't get involved in the kind of relationship you're thinking of.'

Again he laughed.

'Are you,' she responded with sarcasm, 'happy in your work?'

'Crazy about it,' he answered mockingly, 'especially when there's a beautiful girl at my side to share its delights with me. By the way, Anona what?'

'Anona Willis.'

'Willis.'

'That's right.' She smiled impishly. 'Shall I spell it for you? Maybe, under that polished manner'——he shot her a quizzical look,—'you're really an illiterate.'

'How perceptive can you get?' he drawled sarcastically. 'I left school even more ignorant than when I started.'

She smiled. 'You're lying, of course. It's obvious you've been educated.' He inclined his head, still mocking her. 'To quite a high standard, I'd say,' she added.

He gazed thoughtfully at the road ahead. 'Have you been educated to a high standard, as you call it?'

'I'm not in your intellectual league,' she answered flatly. 'I'm a——' She corrected herself. 'I was a secretary in a bank. Now I'm my father's assistant. Also his house-keeper, his secretary and his car driver.' Banishing her seriousness, she swung her head in his direction. 'What are you?'

'What am I? What do you think I am? A drop-out,' he

said with a flicker of a smile. 'Isn't that obvious? I took all
the State had to offer me right up the academic scale in the
way of educating my brain, then, instead of putting my
foot on the lowest rung of the ladder of commerce and in-
dustry, I opted out and became a truck driver.'

She frowned. 'You must be joking.'

'Am I?' was all he answered.

Anona sensed an alteration in the speed of the truck.
Puzzled, she asked, 'What's happening?'

'There's another service station ahead which has public
telephones. I can ring the garage from there and get them
to go out to your car and tow it in.' He smiled, pulling
the vehicle around and parking it. 'Don't tell me you've
forgotten all about it?'

She coloured, hating to admit that she had. He said
with amusement, 'Do you find me so fascinating that
everything else has been pushed out of your head?'

'No!' she exclaimed. She had so nearly said 'yes'.

He laughed again and his reply left her gasping. 'That's
a pity,' he remarked, 'because I find you captivating.' He
leaned forward and across her to open a compartment
under the dashboard not far from her left knee. He extracted a shirt. As he straightened, he turned his head and,
taking her completely by surprise, placed a fleeting kiss on
her lips. He moved upright and, with a gleam in his eyes
at her indignant glare, said, 'As sweet as I thought. Your ex-
fiancé must have been mad to give up the pleasures you
could offer a man.'

'Do you know what you are, Mr——' She wished she
knew his surname.

'Tell me,' he encouraged, pulling on the shirt and
leaving it unbuttoned. B-r-o-d-i-e-s, it said, in scarlet
lettering on the top pocket. His broad shoulders stretched
under the material, his tan stood out against the white of
the shirt. 'No,' he continued, 'I'll save you the trouble. I'm
presumptuous, impudent, audacious. Too bad,' as she
nodded, 'because, given time and even without encourage-

ment, I have every intention of becoming even more presumptuous, etcetera. Why,' with his hand on the door catch, 'do you think I followed you for all those miles? Because I had to know if the front of that irritating woman driver who drove so delicately was as good as the back of her. I can answer the question you haven't yet asked. It was.' His door swung wide and he climbed down.

As he started to walk away, she called through the open window, 'Please Mr—Shane, I'd like to——' he turned, 'like to——' He walked slowly back.

'I said you were delicate, didn't I?'

Turning pink, she waited while he opened the door. Following his instructions, she climbed down backwards into his waiting arms. They crossed over in front of her, crushing her breasts. It was an intimate gesture which might have been born of a familiarity arising from a close relationship lasting for months instead of an acquaintance barely an hour old.

All her past teachings implored her to tear herself free and to rebuke him for his audacity, but her treacherous feelings won the struggle and she lay against him, compliant and unashamedly willing. A low laugh deep in his throat told her of his pleasure at having so easily—as it seemed to him—aroused her lustful feelings and at once her anger stirred to life.

At that moment he released her, only to move his hands to her waist and turn her to face him. She looked stormily up into his triumphantly smiling face and wanted to shout in self-defence, I'm not as easy to get as you think. It's just that there's something about you ...

Irritably she shook herself free and attempted to bring the situation back to normality. 'Besides the—other thing,' she said, succeeding at last in quelling her fast-beating heart, 'I want to call my father. He'll soon start worrying.'

He nodded, detached now and puzzlingly distant after those fleeting, intimate moments. She started on her way to the washroom, glancing back once, only to find him watching her narrowly. Then he turned and made his way to the phone booths.

To Anona's dismay she discovered in the washroom that a coin was needed. She searched in vain in her purse for the correct amount. There was only one thing to do and that was to find Shane and ask him ...

After asking the way, she found the phone booth and saw Shane's tall figure leaning against the side. He was talking emphatically and with a strange kind of authority. Since Anona could not wait until his conversation had ended, she opened the door and heard him say.

'Listen, Rob, I want this whole matter expedited. Have the car towed to the garage and put in the repair bay. Put the best mechanic on to it. I want all the faults listed before I——'

He listened, then went on, 'Yes, I know exactly who she is. She's not royalty, far from it, but for reasons I can't explain now, I want this matter treated as urgent. Get it? Why?' he said impatiently. 'Because——'

He must have sensed that he was being overheard because he turned quickly. 'Yes?' he asked. His good humour had vanished.

Taken aback, she said. 'I haven't any——' and she held out her purse. 'I need——' She told him the coin. Her embarrassment seemed to revive his good humour and he laughed, raking in his pocket. 'Here,' he pulled out a coin, 'will this do?'

She gave him a grateful smile and ran towards the washrooms. By the time she had returned to the phone booth he was waiting outside it.

'I kept this one for you,' he said. She thanked him and looked in her purse again, extracting some coins. 'So you've got the right money this time?' he queried.

She nodded vigorously and began to dial. He propped himself against the open door. She had hoped he would exercise some tact and leave her but, despite the meaningful look she gave him, he ignored the hint. She had no choice but to speak to Mrs Patterson in his hearing, asking the woman to explain the situation to her father.

'Tell him not to worry, will you, if I get home a good bit later than I expected?'

'Do you want to speak to him, dear?' Mrs Patterson asked.

'Don't trouble him,' Anona answered, 'just as long as he knows.' She rang off, saying to the man still leaning indolently against the door, 'I've finished. I hope you found my conversation entertaining.'

He gave a broad grin and walked by her side to the truck. The name 'Brodie' was painted across the front of the truck. She could not get away from the name.

'Brodie's,' she said, putting as much scorn into her voice as she could manage.

'You don't like us?' he asked in a lazy tone.

'Shouldn't you have said "them", since you're just an employee?'

'Ah, but I've worked for them for so many years I feel I almost belong.' His smile faded. 'There's one thing they've done that I admire them for. They've stood out against the big organisations, the take-overs, the monopoly men. They're still a family firm and, I hope, will stay that way into the foreseeable future.'

'You really do have their interests at heart,' she responded, with an attempt at sarcasm.

'You can say that again,' he commented, opening the passenger door and helping her up into the passenger seat. Soon they were on the move once more. Some miles farther on, he slowed down to leave the motorway, forking left. After a while he said, 'In one of those compartments there's a supply of sandwiches and coffee. A short distance ahead there's a parking place. We'll share what there is to eat.' He glanced at her. 'Like the idea?'

'The food and drink's for you. Anyway,' she lied, 'I'm not very hungry.'

Again he showed considerable skill in pulling the long,

large vehicle into a small space. 'You aren't?' he queried. 'After a buttered scone, one cake and one cup of coffee, instead of the proper meal you should have had back there at that restaurant, I'd make a guess that you're famished.'

'I couldn't afford anything more,' she said flatly. 'After a year and a half of living on my father's very small income, plus whatever he gets in social security payments, there's not much left for luxuries like expensive meals.'

He leant across to reach the compartment below the dashboard and in doing so, his shoulder pressed against her. She drew herself in as far as she could, afraid that the pressure of him would once again bring to life her deepest longings. But her efforts to give him more room were plainly not enough. Or was he doing it on purpose?

The sight of the solid muscle of his shoulder, neck and head so close to her face had the blood racing round her like a river in full spate. When would he be finished and let her heart beat at its normal pace again? As he extracted the plastic box, vacuum flask and cups, he turned his head and let his eyes wander slowly over the inviting shape of her. Then his grey eyes lifted to look indolently into the sparkling blue of hers.

'I beg your pardon, Miss Willis,' he said mockingly, 'but the feel of you went straight to my head, like the taste of potent spirits.'

He straightened at last and handed her the box. 'Help yourself. Eat the lot, if you like. My appetite——' his eyes skimmed her flustered face, untidy hair and ruffled blouse, 'one of my appetites, was appeased back there at that restaurant.'

Anona took a sandwich, liked the taste and bit deeply into it. The second mouthful followed in record time, and then the next. He was busy pouring the coffee and she did not think he had noticed until he remarked, 'Not hungry, you said? As I thought, you're ravenous.'

'I'm very sorry,' she said, holding out the box. 'Please

have one. More than one. They're yours, really.'

He waved them away. 'I told you, I've eaten. And I make a point of never over-eating.'

Her eyes dropped automatically to his lean waist topped by no spare flesh at all. She suppressed the ripple of feeling the contemplation of his body had aroused and chewed even harder on the piece of sandwich in her mouth. He passed her a mug of coffee and she nodded her thanks.

He said, having taken a few sips of his coffee, 'What happened to bring your father to his present situation?' He gazed through the windscreen watching a bird flutter over the momentarily empty road ahead. Anona saw it, too. If it doesn't get out of the way quickly, she thought, as a car swished by, it will be killed. She held her breath. It was trapped beneath the car. As the vehicle passed, the bird darted noisily away. It had had a lucky escape.

'You mean how did he come to be confined to a wheel-chair? I told you, one of Brodie's——'

'I know that. I said what happened?'

'By profession, he's a—he was a university professor.'

'Subject?' He tipped back his head and drained the mug dry.

'Archaeology. It was during the winter vacation. He had gone out to buy Christmas presents. He said he was wondering what to buy when he stepped—or so he told witnesses at the time—on to the road. He admitted that out of the corner of his eye he had seen a red truck approaching but thought he could make it in time. He must have misjudged its speed, I suppose, and its ability to brake quickly.'

Having waited for a moment for some reaction—which was not forthcoming—she went on, 'Brodie's denied responsibility, especially since my father had admitted to being in the wrong. They handed the whole matter over to their insurance company. I'm surprised you didn't hear about it, since you're one of their employees.'

He said quietly, 'Truck drivers are more often away, even abroad, than at home.'

'So it could have happened while you were away.'

'More coffee?' he asked, eyebrows raised.

She nodded, handing him her mug which he filled and gave back. She wrapped her hands around its warmth as though the weather was as cold as the season in which her father's accident had happened.

'We received nothing,' she went on, 'no compensation, not even an *ex gratia* payment by the firm to recompense my father for loss of earnings or myself for having to give up my job to look after him.'

Shane was putting away the empty food box and vacuum flasks. 'Couldn't he have continued with his work, lecturing from his wheelchair?'

Anona shook her head. 'Field work is involved—going out to archaeological sites, taking part in digs for ancient remains. Not to mention travelling to London and back every day. He resigned from his job. We decided to move to Derbyshire which he's always loved, even though his accident happened there.'

She sighed and stared unseeingly across the fields. 'Now he's writing a book,' she continued, 'on his past travels across the world. I'm helping him. He's got a publisher waiting for it, luckily, but my father's so methodical it's taking a long time to complete the book.'

Shane bent down to put away the food containers. He made no attempt to touch her this time; his mind appeared to be on other things. After checking over his shoulder and again in the driving and wing mirrors, he turned the steering wheel, arm over arm, hand over hand, swinging the wheel back to straighten out the vehicle on the open road.

'You drive,' Anona commented, 'as if you've been doing it for years.'

'I told you, I have, ever since the law allowed me to. By

the way, did I also tell you that I've made arrangements for your car to be towed to a garage and inspected?'

She did not think it wise to inform him that she had overheard his conversation with a man called Rob. 'Thanks,' she said, then frowned. 'Will it be expensive?'

'Who knows? They'll give an estimate of the cost.'

'I've got to have a car for my father's sake. He'd go mad if he never got out of the house, which is what it would mean if I didn't have one.' She sighed and was silent for a while, staring at the passing countryside. 'Since I can't afford to buy another car, no matter how much the repairs cost I'll have to find the money somehow.'

Her companion drove steadily, making no comment. His shirt flapped open in the breeze which came in through the open window. Why, she wondered with alarm, did her pulse rate increase at the sight, even the mere thought, of him? She had only met him about two hours before, yet the man had made an impact on her which she would never forget.

His competence was beyond doubt. The tormentor who had hung on to her tail all those miles along the motorway had gone, leaving in his place a driver with skill, lightning-fast reactions and total concentration. With surprise she realised that, even on the basis of her short acquaintance with him, she trusted him implicitly.

Over the sound of the engine she said, 'You've been very kind, Shane. Doing so much to help me ... I don't know how to thank you.'

A swift glance skimmed over her and he gazed at the road again with a smile. 'Shall I find another layby and demonstrate how that could be done? Quite simple,' he said, changing gear to climb a hill, 'this,' a finger to his mouth, 'meeting this,' without looking and with his free hand he found her lips, tantalising her yet again with his touch. 'Or are you mean with your kisses? Is that why your boy-friend broke off the engagement?'

'*I* broke it off,' she said indignantly. He smiled and they both lapsed into silence again. Later, he said, 'Do you want to know why I've been so kind?' She nodded, her eyes opening in expectation of the compliment that was to come. 'Once truck drivers, the old-fashioned kind, used to be called the knights of the road, helping anyone in trouble. Maybe,' with a broad smile, 'I'm just plain old-fashioned.'

'Oh.'

He must have heard the flatness of her tone because he laughed. He did not speak, thus leaving her to face her own vanity and hurt pride. She had expected personal praise which, from the man beside her, would have meant a great deal to her. Acknowledging this fact set up such a chain of anxiety reaction within her—she really would never see him again after he had dropped her and gone on his way—that she was silent for many miles.

At last her companion spoke again. 'How long did you say you've been away?'

'A week.'

'A whole week to break off an engagement?'

'That only took me a couple of days. It wasn't very pleasant.' Involuntarily she felt for her empty finger. 'It's not something I'd recommend.' Her head turned. 'Have you ever——'

He answered with mock solemnity, 'No, I haven't ever.'

'The rest of the time,' Anona went on, 'after I signed the papers, I looked up old friends to say my goodbyes all over again.'

'You sound as if you didn't enjoy your week.' She shook her head. 'Had you lived in the house long?'

'I was born there. Altogether, my parents lived there for twenty-five years. My mother died six years ago when I was eighteen.' She looked at the hills which rose invitingly on both sides and sighed with contentment. 'It's good to be back.'

'So you like Derbyshire?'

'Very much. We became attached to the place after

we'd spent some camping holidays in the area. My father decided then that it was the place he wanted to retire to one day. About three years ago he bought a cottage, intending that we should use it as a holiday home. We live there now.'

'At the time of the accident you were spending Christmas here?'

'We came whenever we could, regardless of the season or the weather.'

He asked her where she lived and she told him. 'That's only a couple of miles from Brodie's depot,' he said, 'so I'll drop you outside your home.'

She told him there was no need, but he insisted. The sound of the truck echoed enormously between the stone houses of the village street. She wished she had the courage to ask him not to stop directly outside their cottage. She did not know what her father's reaction would be to her arriving home in a vehicle owned by the company which had deprived him of so much in life.

She wondered if her companion had read her mind because when she said, 'Please put me down here,' he answered, his jaw hardening, 'I'm taking you all the way.'

It was beyond her understanding why a mere employee should be so quick to defend his employers, as the firmness of his tone had implied. 'There,' she said, pointing to a stone-built cottage with a red-tiled roof. 'It looks a bit tumbledown, but it's cosy inside and clean, which is——'

He braked and interrupted with a faintly amused smile, 'I don't live in a palace myself, so stop falling over yourself to apologise.'

Something in his tone, that suggestion of arrogance and authority she had detected in the phone booth, made her colour quickly. She gave in to her instinct to retaliate. 'There's no need to be patronising! It's not my father's fault that he's unable to afford better.'

He looked surprised by her outburst. 'Who's patronising?' he asked. And when his words repeated themselves in her mind, she had to acknowledge that he was right.

'Sorry.' She gathered up her belongings and attempted to open the door. He was climbing out of the cab and walking round to her side of the truck before she could do so. He took her cases and coat, putting them down, then his hands went up to catch her round the waist. He swung her from the top steps to the ground and twirled her round to face him. She gazed up at him, her smile uncertain. She thought he was waiting for an expression of gratitude, but all she said was, 'Thanks.'

Still his hands spanned her waist. 'I enjoyed your company,' he said.

She smiled provocatively up at him. 'Better than listening to dedications and loving messages with music on the truck radio?'

'Much, much better. A real live girl beside me. A blonde, too,' his finger flicked a stray curl, 'with smiling blue eyes, an impudent nose and wide, inviting lips.'

She could not stop the quick colour. Her eyes dropped to his chest, revealed by his now partially buttoned shirt. There was an almost irresistible urge to press her fingers against the hardness of him, to reach out to the private person beneath the tough, power-orientated outward appearance of the man.

'Shall we translate your thanks into action?'

'You mean,' her long-lashed eyes gazed into his, 'that I should give you a——'

'I'm not stealing.' His eyes, which had the bewildering ability to change in two seconds from cold detachment to genuine amusement, were laughing at her. 'No fiancé now to punch me on the chin for taking what's his.'

Before she could protest, his lips were on hers, cool yet firm, hinting at an ocean-depth of feeling beneath the calm surface. It did not last, that kiss, but it was enough to bring her hand up swiftly to wipe away his touch.

'What's wrong?' he asked, letting her go. 'Afraid to be

seen being kissed by a truck driver? Would it lower your status in the eyes of your neighbours?'

His sarcasm pained her. 'I'm no snob! It's just that if my father saw, how do you think he'd feel, when it was a Brodie's vehicle which knocked him down?'

He climbed up into the driving seat, started the engine and called over the noise,

'I'll let you know about your car,' and was on his way.

CHAPTER THREE

ANONA used her key to let herself into the cottage. It had been built in the early nineteenth century and a few alterations had been made. Since her father had bought the place before his accident and when his income had been good, he had engaged the services of a reputable local builder to make the cottage weather-proof and free of damp.

The windows had been modernised but not so much as to spoil the overall appearance of the stone-built dwelling. The front door was now of glass instead of heavy wood. The small entrance lobby led to the living-room which contained wall-to-wall carpeting, comfortable chairs covered in heavy floral fabric and a solid, highly-polished wooden table.

There was a warm smile of welcome from her father as she entered. His glasses were in place and his grey hair and beard were neatly combed. He looked, in fact, as though there was nothing wrong with him and that at any moment he wished, he could lift himself out of the wheelchair and walk across the room. It almost broke Anona's heart to know that he would never, without crutches, be able to take such an action again.

Her father waited expectantly as she sank on to the thick-tufted hearthrug not far from his chair. 'You look very pretty, my dear,' he commented. 'Did your car decide to behave itself after all and bring you all those miles home?'

Was she looking as bright as he had said? If so, she wondered with alarm what the reason might be. The answer was obvious, but she refused to acknowledge it. She would never see the truck driver again. He had promised to let her know the verdict on her car, but it would probably be a garage mechanic who contacted her.

She answered her father's question, shaking her head. 'I left it looking very lonely on the hard shoulder of the motorway. I don't know what I would have done if a driver hadn't come to my aid.'

'A car driver? I expect it was your pretty face and helpless look that made him stop.'

'Not a car driver, Father.' She tugged gently at the tufts of the handmade rug which her mother had made years before. 'A truck driver pulled in and——' she could not tell him the whole story, 'and looked inside the engine, but he couldn't do anything. So he brought me all the way home.'

'How very kind of him. But wasn't it out of his way?'

She shook her head and went on, hoping to distract her father's attention, 'He phoned a garage and arranged for them to tow the car to their repair department. They promised to examine it and give an estimate of the cost.'

'A modern-day Sir Galahad on four wheels!' her father exclaimed with a delighted chuckle.

'*Four* wheels? You should have seen the monster he was driving! Fourteen wheels is more like it. And,' she smoothed down the tufts she had brushed upright, 'he said that truck drivers used to be known as the knights of the road because they helped so many people——' she stole a glance at her father's smiling face, 'especially pretty girls.'

Was he in a good enough mood to take the information she had so far withheld? 'He drove a Brodie's truck, Father.'

Will Willis's face lost its amusement. 'You accepted a lift in a Brodie's vehicle? After what they did to me?'

'I had no choice,' she said in anguish. 'I might have been standing by the car even now if I hadn't. People were driving by me as if I didn't exist.' The anger had not left her father's face. 'Anyway, the man was an employee. It wasn't his fault if one of his colleagues was responsible for the accident, was it? And he did get me home safely.'

The condemning frown still had not left her father's face. 'He did so much for me, Father, made those arrangements about the car, gave me his sandwiches when he——' she could not mention the incident in the restaurant, 'he discovered I hadn't eaten much lunch.' It seemed that her words were beginning to pacify her father.

'I must admit it sounds as if he was very thoughtful. Of course,' he observed, his tension ebbing, 'I have a lot of admiration for truck drivers. I don't envy them their jobs, hauling heavy loads from one side of the country to the other.'

Anona relaxed as her father relented, although, she thought, why she should want to defend the particular truck driver who had helped her, she did not know.

'I don't know whether you've noticed,' she said, changing the subject, 'but——' she held out her empty hand, 'I've broken off my engagement.'

Her father showed immediate concern. 'Anona, my dear —I hope that I was not the cause?'

Anona assured him that he was not. 'It was a mistake, on my part, anyway. I felt there was something wrong when I didn't miss Dougal. I thought I'd long for him night and day.' She lifted her shoulders. 'It just didn't happen.'

'Was Dougal upset?'

'I think so, at first. He seemed to recover fairly quickly, though. We agreed to remain friends.'

There was a familiar tap on the door and the next-door neighbour came in. Her welcome for Anona was warm and she listened with interest as Anona told her about the car and lift in the truck. Mrs Patterson agreed that the young man who had gone to her rescue couldn't be blamed for an accident which another of Brodie's drivers had caused. Reluctantly Will Willis allowed himself to be persuaded to her point of view.

'Will the car take long to mend, dear?' Mrs Patterson

asked. 'My husband used to be handy with mending such things, but I think he's past the age for lying on the ground face up, with the top half of him hidden underneath a car!'

They laughed and Professor Willis said, 'As long as the car's not too old to merit spending good money on it ...' He sighed. 'But even if it takes all our savings we'll have to have it repaired. Another car, even a secondhand one, is out of the question.'

'And you have to have a car, don't you, Will?' Mrs Patterson sympathised, 'otherwise you're almost a prisoner in your own house.'

Something made Anona say hurriedly, 'Oh, I'm sure that if it's humanly possible to mend the car, Sh——Mr——' She did not know his surname! 'Shane will see that it's done.'

'So it's first names, is it?' said Mrs Patterson, winking at Will from her armchair opposite him. 'Wait until I tell my Kenny what a fast worker our Anona is!'

Anona laughed uncomfortably, unwilling to confess to the real reason why she was forced to refer to the man by his first name—that he plainly hadn't thought it worth-while telling his passenger his other name.

All day Anona waited for a phone call, and all day it did not come. When her father asked her when she expected to hear 'the worst', as he put it, she managed a careless shrug. 'In a day or two. You know what garage workshops are like. They get a car brought in, but they have so much work on hand they put it to one side.' In fact, she not only convinced her father, she convinced herself, too.

Shane had merely said, 'I'll let you know about your car.' He had not specified a time. He hadn't even told her where her car was being taken. It could be miles away, even at that moment.

The second day passed without a word from him. When the third day arrived, she could not bear it any longer. 'I'll call Brodie's,' she told her father. 'I'll see if I can at least speak to Sh—— to the man himself.'

'Unlikely, Anona,' Will said. 'He could be hundreds of miles away across Europe, or in the wilds of northern Scotland!'

Silently she agreed, but she was feeling so disillusioned about the man called Shane—the fact that he seemed to have forgotten her existence, let alone her car's, forgotten, too, his promise to contact her—that she could not allow another day to pass without trying to obtain some kind of news.

Brodie's head office number she knew by heart from her dealings with the haulage firm in the past. Since she did not know of any other way to make personal contact with one of their employees, she was compelled to call the head office first.

When her call was answered with a 'Brodie's, can I help you?' Anona swallowed her embarrassment and said, 'Can—can I speak to—to one of your drivers, please? He's called Shane, and——'

'I'm sorry,' said the girl at head office, 'would you repeat that?'

'I said, his name is Shane, and I wondered if——'

'Excuse me, madam,' had the girl's voice and manner altered? 'you did say Shane?' Anona answered yes, she did. 'Well, I'm sorry, but I have to ask you this, but would you be one of this gentlemen's friends—lady friends?'

'No, I wouldn't!' Anona replied indignantly. 'I just want to know what's happened about——'

'No need to explain, madam,' the girl cut in smoothly. 'I'll see if I can find him for you.'

With a frown and a sinking of the heart—had the man taken her in completely, with his charm and his kiss and his 'arrangements' about the repairs, and had she seen the last of her precious car for ever?—Anona waited to hear whether the girl had managed to trace him.

'Who is it?' The curt voice in her ear made her jump,

jabbing at her ragged nerves and setting her pulses beating
alarmingly fast.

It was Authority speaking this time, no indulgent
humour in sight, nor even mild mockery. Where did that
authority come from, and what gave him the right to
speak in such a way?

'It's——' she cleared her throat, 'it's Anona, Anona
Willis.'

A few seconds passed before he made a response. When
he did, it was as though another man was speaking. 'Ah,
the girl in distress I plucked from the rapacious jaws of
the motorway. I imagine it's the state of your car you're
enquiring about?'

Bewildered by the apparent personality change in the
space of only a few seconds, Anona said, child-like, 'Yes,
please.'

'Well,' it sounded as though there was a smile on his
face, 'I've had the estimate.'

'You said you would phone me.' There was a note of
reproach she could not suppress.

'Yes, well, there were a number of reasons. To put it
bluntly, it's going to cost you a small fortune.'

'But Shane,' she wailed, 'we haven't got that kind of
money! I told you——'

'I haven't forgotten.' Was there a return of the merest
hint of brusqueness? He went on in yet another tone-
change, 'Are you free this evening?'

'I'm free every evening—that is, when my father can
spare me.'

'Then come to Brodie's filling station and repair depot at
around seven and we'll talk about it.'

'There's nothing to talk about, is there? I might as
well get whatever I can for my car as scrap.'

'I told you,' he went on with forced patience, 'come
round this evening. Shall I call for you?'

'Would it be in a Brodie's truck?'

'What would you prefer—a Rolls-Royce?'

'Who wouldn't?' She took a breath. 'Better not, Shane. My father was a bit upset when I told him about the lift you gave me in a Brodie's vehicle the other day. I persuaded him in the end that it couldn't possibly have been your fault that the accident happened, because you're just another employee. I think he accepted the argument. But I don't think he'd appreciate the sight of a Brodie's truck outside the door again, and me climbing into it.'

The response was so long in coming she asked, 'Are you still there?'

'I'm still here. You'll have to find your own way to the garage in that case, won't you? Until seven.' He rang off before she could thank him.

When Anona walked across the courtyard of Brodie's filling station, she did so hesitantly. It seemed the self-service pumps were still open as cars were being fed from them, the car owners making their way to the glass-fronted shop to pay their bills.

Anona waited in the line as if she, too, had filled her car tank. When it was her turn, the young woman operating the till looked at her enquiringly.

'Excuse me,' said Anona, 'but could you tell me where I'd find a man called—I mean, one of Brodie's drivers called Shane?'

'Shane?' The young woman looked at her with such interest Anona was glad she had changed from her old check shirt and jeans into a summer dress. 'Would your name be Anona?'

'Yes, it is. How strange that you should guess it.'

The girl gave her an odd look and said, pointing, 'Go out of here, round the back, then walk straight ahead and you can't miss the repair workshop. It's big enough.'

Anona thanked her and made for the door. The evening was warm but with a breeze which had come down from the hills and gave warning of the sun's disappearance behind them. At the rear of the filling station shop was a snack bar. Beyond that a large area stretched where trucks stood neatly in line in various stages of repair. All were scarlet and all bore the name Brodie in large letters. Here and there stood private cars as if waiting for collection by their owners.

To the left of the open space was a covered area with a wide-spanning sloping roof. It was there that she saw her car. Jutting out from beneath it were two long legs. She walked up to the car and regarded it uncertainly. She cleared her throat and said, 'Excuse me.'

The two legs stiffened, then bent at the knees and finally the rest of the person appeared. A few moments later, the man called Shane towered above her. Anona had not expected such a surge of pleasure at the sight of him. The fact that it happened after such a short acquaintance both alarmed yet electrified her.

'Miss Willis,' he said, smiling broadly, and holding out his hand. 'It's good to renew our acquaintance.'

Her eyes searched his face, seeking for mockery. Yes, it was there in his eyes as it had been in his voice. She put out her hand automatically to take his. He gripped her hand tightly, then released it, laughing.

'Oh——' she said, exasperated, 'now look!' She displayed her grease-covered hand. 'You did that deliberately!'

'So that I could have the pleasure of removing it.' He found a rag and opened a bottle containing a strong-smelling liquid, moistened the cloth and lifted her hand. With a stroking action, he began to remove the black grease. His eyes found hers, looking into them, his half-smile hinting at thoughts which made her heart beat painfully.

When the grease was removed she thanked him, then looked round for a wash-basin.

'I'll show you later where to wash,' he remarked, wiping his own hands on the moistened rag. He looked her over, plainly liking the lavender-and-white freshness of her dress, liking even more the hidden, yet hinted at, attractions beneath it. As if he could not resist, his finger approached a coil of curls.

She drew back, her reaction fast. 'Not with greasy hands,' she protested.

'Meaning,' his eyebrows lifted, 'that it must wait until my hands are clean?'

'I meant no such thing!' she retorted, and his head went back in laughter. She looked at her car, saying, 'It's nice to see it again. Why were you underneath it?'

'Putting finishing touches to the repairs.'

'*Finishing* touches? But Shane, I told you I couldn't afford to pay a lot of money. How could you go ahead and have the repairs carried out when you knew——'

He held up his hands, still smeared here and there with grease. 'I said I was putting the finishing touches to it.'

'So who did the work?' she asked, bewildered. She noted the long-sleeved, zip-fronted overall he wore, with the name Brodie embroidered across one side of the chest. 'You?'

'Don't sound so surprised. I told you, didn't I, that I was born with a silver spanner in my hand, or my mouth. I forget which. I repair all vehicles, cars, motor-cycles, even the firm's trucks when I have the time. There are the regular mechanics, of course, but I help out in emergencies and so on. It's a hobby of mine.'

She frowned. 'But aren't you employed as a driver?'

'If a truck breaks down, say miles, even hundreds of miles, from nowhere, and a driver has no knowledge of mechanics and repair work, do you think he's going to abandon his vehicle, which in itself may have cost his firm thousands in money, not to mention a valuable load which belongs to another company?'

'Which means he has to do his own repairs if he can?'

Shane shrugged. 'If he can't, either he has to thumb a lift to the nearest phone box or,' with a smile, 'if he's crossing a desert, as some of them do, request a lift on a passing camel.'

Anona laughed and Shane's eyes lingered on her bright eyes and pink cheeks. 'So you've repaired my car?' she remarked. 'It was very kind of you.'

Eyebrows lifted. 'Was it?'

She nodded. 'Now will you please send your bill to me, not to my father? I hope——' she passed the back of her fingers over her lips, 'I mean I——'

'You hope it's not too expensive.'

He had guessed her thoughts, but she denied the statement with a quick shake of the head. 'I was going to say I hope you don't mind if—if it takes me a little while to pay it. If——' Would she embarrass him if she went on? 'If you need the money, maybe I can find some way to pay you——'

He smiled. 'I think a wash and a cup of tea would be welcome, don't you?'

She let out a breath and nodded. He put his two hands to each side of her head and moved it backwards and forwards. 'Always nodding, aren't you? Always saying "yes".'

'No!' He laughed. 'And please remove your greasy hands from my hair!'

'It looks virgin-clean and,' he bent down, 'sweet-smelling. What male can resist putting a first footmark on to untouched snow? Or,' softly, 'virgin territory?'

'I'm not a vir——' Hastily she stopped.

There was the faintest narrowing of his eyes. 'You're not? I was forgetting you've been an engaged woman.'

Her eyes lifted wide, blue and challenging. 'Did you have to buy spare parts to mend my car?'

The swift change of subject seemed to amuse him. 'Whatever was needed we had in stock.'

'Which means that as a Brodie's employee you had to pay for them and that means I owe you some money.'

'Not forgetting the discount for staff,' he added, the faint smile lingering.

'I don't mind if you don't pass the discount on. I'm

very grateful to you for all you've done.'

'I'll send in my bill.' There was a glint in his eyes which made her wonder if he was laughing at her.

'Please do. When will my car be finished?'

'Tomorrow. I'll deliver it to your door.'

'I'd rather collect it, thanks.'

As she turned to go, head high, he said softly, 'Come down off your pedestal, Miss Willis.'

Remembering all he had done for her—and temporarily forgetting the way he had dogged her tire marks on the motorway for mile after mile—she said, her manner softening, 'What time of day will you come?'

His smile was hidden by his swing away from her, making for a door which appeared to lead into a small room. 'Evening. Eightish. Okay?'

Following him, she said it was. Looking around the room which had a tumbledown air, hooks on the walls, empty diesel oil cans, beer cans and water pipes draped with dirty rags, she said eight o'clock would be fine. In the corner was a wash-basin with taps.

'Is this where I wash?' she asked, looking at her grimy hands.

He smiled. 'Sink, dirty towel, taps, but no hot water. So no, it isn't the place for a lady to wash.' He zipped open his overall, stepped out of it and hung it on an empty hook. His short-sleeved shirt was open at the neck, his jeans oil-stained and patched.

Yet when she raised her head and looked at the impressive build, the fine features and the intelligent eyes, she sensed once again that something about him did not add up. Truck driver, skilled mechanic—yet he preferred to eat, not at a low-priced café but at a high-priced restaurant, with all the trimmings. Ability to manipulate a giant truck, yet a command of his mother-tongue and an ease of self-expression which spoke of a trained and educated mind ...

He smiled, seizing her hand. 'Having made an exhaustive diagnosis of my personality and no doubt torn it into shreds, come with me, my girl by the wayside from which I plucked you. Remind me to wear you in my buttonhole.'

It was impossible not to smile back. One greasy hand in another, they swung across the parking area for broken-down trucks and cars, making for the café behind the shop. Shane reached in his pocket for a bunch of keys, selected one and opened the main entrance door.

Anona looked up at him, puzzled. 'Do Brodie's issue every one of their truck drivers with a full set of keys?'

He glanced at her quickly. 'Hardly. I have to live somewhere, hence I carry a multitude of keys.'

The answer did not satisfy her completely, but her companion did not seem to care. He pulled her behind him, past the back of the service counter and into the kitchens at the rear. They walked on and into a small room with two other doors. The keys appeared again and each door was unlocked.

'You wash here——' he looked up, pointing, 'as the sign indicates. I wash there. Okay?'

Anona nodded and went on her way. When she emerged, clean, refreshed and with newly-combed hair, he had the kettle boiling and cups placed on saucers. His hair had been combed, too. The jeans had been replaced by well-fitting brown slacks, the working shirt with a blue polo-necked shirt.

A teapot stood on a table and Anona watched while her host spooned tea into it, then poured on the boiling water. He rested a thigh against a working top and her puzzlement grew at his relaxed, unselfconscious, almost autocratic manner.

His smile this time was sardonic. 'Work on it, Miss Willis. You'll get there in the end.'

'Get where?'

He answered not with words but with a smile. Embarrassed, she looked around and subjected her surroundings to the same scrutiny.

'Impressed?' he asked.

'By the cleanliness, the modern equipment? Very.'

'Good. We aim to satisfy all regulations, even to better them.'

'We?'

His eyes narrowed. 'You're quick, Miss Willis. Brodie's, of course. Even if I am a mere truck driver, I have that elusive thing that's so lacking in life today—loyalty to one's firm.'

It was an explanation, and since she had no other option, she was forced to accept it. 'The tea—shall I pour?' A movement of his hand invited her to do so. He took a cup but refused sugar. He invited her to sit down which she did, at the table.

For a few minutes there was silence. Although she kept her eyes averted from him, she knew he was looking at her. This made her feel uncomfortable and with a finger she traced the name on the sugar packet. The girl in the shop adjoining the café had stared when she had answered to the name Anona. Why? And how had the girl known her name?

'Shane?' He helped himself to more tea, after offering her some which she refused. 'Are your parents living in this area?'

'Yes,' he said abruptly. It was a warning which clearly said, 'Keep out.'

She changed her tactics. 'You told me you were unmarried. I can't understand it.' She looked up at him, smiling. 'Maybe you're divorced?'

'I'm not, and never have been, tied to any woman.'

In the few moments that she analysed his words, he crossed to the table and put down his cup. 'Ah,' she said at last, 'that means there have been women, but——'

The slight sound could have been a long-suffering sigh

or exasperation. 'Aren't you treading on dangerous ground? What am I supposed to read into your questions?'

She stood up irritably, as much annoyed with herself for probing as with him for his subtle warning.

'Maybe,' he went on, 'you're really querying my virility? I can reassure you on that point here and now.'

He closed the gap between them and she felt against her the light pressure of his body. For a few seconds he stood there, giving her every chance to move away. But she was trapped—by her own awakening desires; by his nearness which was revealing to her small details about his face—the cheekbones beneath dark, deepset eyes, the shadowy darkness around his jaw and upper lip which must, if she dared to raise her hand and touch them, feel rough.

Most of all she was ensnared by the power of his maleness reaching out and enveloping her, even though his hands were still at his sides. Now her body was, of its own accord, being drawn towards his and, as if to catch her, his arms lifted and held her.

'Shane?' she whispered, her fingers pleating the fabric of his shirt.

'Anona?' he responded, his fingers outspreading over her back. His head bent and his lips brushed hers. Her eyes as they searched his must have contained a question because he said softly, 'I told you I found you captivating.'

'That doesn't give you the key to the door where my lips are concerned,' she parried, pushing at him gently.

'Doesn't it?' His eyes opened with false astonishment. 'Well then, if I can't have access to your lips, what about here?' He found her throat, bringing shivers to her tingling body. 'And this?' He pulled aside the neckline of her dress and brushed his mouth across her shoulder, leaving a throbbing trail.

Her breaths came quickly. 'No,' she said, 'no, no!' Her palms pushed in vain at his chest.

'Then these it will have to be,' he answered, and his mouth covered hers. At first she struggled, doing her utmost to twist from his hold. When the essence of his kiss manifested itself on her taste buds, she found that her limbs, her emotions and her will itself had turned traitor and that she was surrendering gladly to the demands of his arms, his hands and his questing, insistent mouth.

A feeling rose inside her that it was all wrong, that such intimacy should not be forming between them. There was no involvement on either side, no friendship, no depth of feeling. Her knowledge of him was minuscule, his knowledge of her even less. All there was was an attraction on his side and—yes, she had to admit it—on hers, too.

All the time she had been thinking, hazily like walking through a cloud, the kiss had been growing in urgency, threatening to demolish her barriers, leaving her vulnerable and entirely at his mercy.

When she felt his hand invade the neckline of her dress, as if it had every right to be there and intended finding out for itself whether the outward promise of her shapeliness was as sweet and enticing as it appeared; when her whole body came alight with pleasure at the stroking touch of him, she knew it would take all her reserves of mental strength to resist him.

There was no weapon at her disposal but to go limp in his arms. This she forced herself to do and he seemed instantly aware of her withdrawal. He let her go, saying tauntingly, 'As I thought—despite your engagement, virgin territory.'

She flared, 'If you're trying to trap me into saying "yes" or "no", you won't succeed. You had no right to do what you've just done!'

'None at all,' he conceded with a lazy smile.

'Anyway, I told you—I've just broken free from one entanglement, and I don't want another.'

'Who's talking about entanglements?'

She was furious with herself for giving him the chance
to put her in her place. 'If you think I'm a casual pick-
up——'

'So, in spite of your statement, it's a permanent relationship you're after? Didn't I tell *you*—no staying power
where such things are concerned?'

Her eyes threw out sparks, her breasts rose and fell with
trapped anger. 'You—you!' she breathed. 'You're so
conceited you really think it's you I want as a permanent
partner?'

'Judging by the way you positively enjoyed my lovemaking,' he said, eyeing her slightly dishevelled appearance, 'I think my conceit, if that's what it is, is justified.'

'You're twisting things again,' she accused. 'Like the
way you alleged I "played cat and mouse" with you on
the motorway, when all I wanted was to get away from
that mad, crazy truck driver who kept following me. Like
the way you didn't believe me when my car broke down
and you thought I wanted you to make love to me in the
back of my own car.'

He smiled at the memory.

'You were wrong then,' she stormed, 'and you're wrong
now.' You're lying, she told herself, you are attracted to
him, this man fascinates you, you dread the moment,
very soon now, when you'll have seen him for the last
time ...

Casually he moved towards her and, with a touch of
intimacy, lifted back into place the neckline of her dress.
His fingers stayed to trail her throat from one side to the
other. Tension stiffened her body and she endeavoured to
suppress her longing for closer contact with him.

She said, the stiffness invading her voice, 'If you'll be
kind enough to bring the car to my father's house tomorrow evening, I'll settle your bill straight away. Thank you
for all you've done.'

Walking round to the front and crossing the courtyard
of the filling station Anona cherished a faint hope that he

might call out to her that he would give her a lift. Here and there were Brodie's vans—it wouldn't have hurt him, she thought irritably, to have used one of those.

Even as she let herself into the cottage, a vague kind of anger still lingered. However, since it was necessary to hide her annoyance from her father—he would demand an explanation which she could not honestly give—she told herself to stop being foolish and her normal good temper prevailed.

All day, a sense of anticipation carried her along. Even while she did her shopping in the village it followed her as if it were on a lead. As she attended to her father's needs, typed his notes, cooked the meals, it enveloped her like a delicately-coloured sari.

When the knock came on the door, she was sitting with her father in the living-room. She ran to the window which overlooked the street and saw her car parked by the curb. A short distance behind it was another car, twice the size of hers and infinitely more powerful.

'It would be a good idea,' said her father a little dryly, 'if you opened the door and saw for yourself who our visitor is.'

The front door opened to reveal a man, tall, thin and wearing an overall. The word 'Brodie' was woven on it in scarlet. The man in the overall, however, was not the man she expected. Her face was smiling for Shane, her close-fitting blue open-necked top and button-through skirt were for Shane. Her hair had been specially washed into a glowing, loosely curling mass of silkiness for Shane. Yet he had not come.

'I've brought your car, miss,' the man said. 'With Brodie's compliments.'

The words of thanks would not come. The frown was of intense disappointment, but the man took them to be puzzlement. 'Nothing to pay,' he added. 'It goes like a bird now.'

At last she found her voice. 'Thank you very much, but I must pay. I can't allow ...' Her voice tailed off, disbelief gripping her. I'll deliver it myself, he had said last night. Eight o'clock, they had agreed. 'Where's the man who was working on it?' she asked. The mechanic looked puzzled. 'The man called Sh——' A car door slammed and a man made his way towards the cottage, walking with easy strides along the garden path.

'Jim,' said the newcomer, 'okay.' With his head he motioned to the large sprawling car parked behind hers. 'Wait, will you? I'll take you back.' The man nodded and passed the new arrival on his return to the roadway.

'Shane?' It was a whisper.

'Who else?' He smiled. At least that hasn't changed, she thought, although everything else has.

'The—the car?' she went on. 'The man.' She indicated Shane's companion. 'You.' She looked him up and down, noting open-eyed the cut and quality of his suit, the neatness yet the strength and bigness—there was no other word—of his bearing. He carried himself like an executive, yet he crawled under cars, getting his hands covered in grease. He drove a monster of a truck, rescued a girl from the roadside and fed her with sandwiches and coffee.

He lunched with the ease of a rich man at a good class restaurant, turning his back on the more modest café invariably patronised by truck drivers. She did not know his surname, yet he had kissed her—she had forgotten how many times. *So who was this man?*

CHAPTER FOUR

HIS eyes travelled the length and breadth of her. They lingered on the curving shape, the glimpse of white throat, the trusting, questing blue eyes, the curling softness of the fair hair.

'I could,' he said softly, 'drink you from a crystal wine glass, eat you from Minton china. I could make a meal of you any day, given the slightest encouragement.'

'Please,' she whispered, fearful that her father might hear the strangely intimate conversation, 'stop talking nonsense. Please tell me what it's all about.'

By now the man called Jim had got into the car Shane had been driving. Shane answered, his hand finding a pocket, 'Nothing to tell. Jim's from Brodie's too. Someone had to drive your car and someone else had to follow to take him back.'

'All right,' she broke in, 'so he's a colleague of yours, but——' she continued to look bewildered, 'you ...' indicating the car, 'that ...'

'Didn't I say,' he answered softly, 'carry on, Miss Willis. You'll get there in the end?'

'Anona!' It was her father calling. 'Show the young man in. Since he's done so much for you, the least you could do is to offer him a drink.'

The quick colour flooded Anona's pale cheeks. 'I'm sorry, I'm not usually inhospitable. Please come in. And,' she looked across to the car, 'your colleague.'

'I'd like to, thanks, but not for long. And Jim—well, I doubt if he'll mind waiting a few minutes.'

Anona's father had manoeuvred his chair into the entrance hall. 'Come in—Shane, isn't it? I've heard nothing else for the past two or three days.'

'Father! You know that's not true.' The colour had come again and Shane, deeply amused, gave Anona a meaningful glance.

'Professor Willis? I'm pleased to make your acquaintance, especially after the build-up your daughter's given you.'

Now Will Willis laughed. 'I have something of a soft spot for my daughter, too. Life wouldn't be worth living without her.'

Hands were extended and shaken and Will moved his chair so that it faced the living-room, then led the way into the room. 'That drink, Shane. What will you have?'

Will, determinedly playing the role of host, despite his disability, reached out to glasses and bottles and, with a steady hand, poured. Anona distributed the glasses and invited their guest to be seated. He was so large he dwarfed the room and its occupants, while his air of complete self-confidence did little to boost her own.

'I'm glad of this chance,' said Professor Willis, 'to thank you. Not only did you rescue my daughter from a very difficult situation, you also mended her car.'

His keen eyes, reflecting an intelligence which had certainly not been dulled by the accident, were doing their best to sum up the intellectual and social status of the slightly formidable specimen of manhood who now leaned back, quite at ease, in the chair on the other side of the fireplace.

The frown told his daughter that he, like herself, had been unsuccessful in his efforts. He was about to speak when the object of his scrutiny replied, smiling at the girl who sat nearby, 'She gave me the pleasure of her company. It was my way of saying "thank you" to her for that.'

Anona smiled back. 'Who taught you to make such pretty speeches, Shane?'

He was unmoved by her playful taunt. 'She doesn't believe me, Professor Willis. Who taught *her* to be so modest?'

The Professor laughed, but Anona asked, 'How much do we owe you, Shane?'

He put his glass down and rose. 'I said,' he ruffled her hair, 'I'd send in my bill.'

With an irritated movement, she smoothed her hair. 'And I want to pay you now.'

'And I haven't done my arithmetic yet. Would you believe me if I said I've even forgotten how to add up?'

Will Willis laughed but Anona frowned, not knowing how to take his evasions. 'Surely even a truck driver has to do his sums sometimes,' she commented, deciding to pretend to take his words at their face value. 'I mean— weight loads, the amount a truck can hold——' His loud laughter stopped her. 'All right, so you've been fooling me. You're not going to tell me how much, are you? But I *insist* on paying.'

A glance at his watch created the diversion he was plainly wanting. 'Jim's waiting. I must take him back.'

Anona grabbed Shane's arm. 'You're not getting out of it that way. How much is it?' His response was to cover her hand with his and gaze, smiling, into her eyes. At once her legs felt weak, her body limp ... She pulled herself together. 'I said how much, Shane?'

'Anona,' her father intervened, 'have you never learnt to accept a gift gracefully?'

'Yes, but——' She tried to withdraw her hand, but it was held fast.

'Fine. You've allowed me to do my good deed.' Shane's fingers tightened over hers. 'In a life which so far has not been over-virtuous, it will stand out like a shining light. Like your smiling face.'

Anona began to panic. All this in front of her father! 'Stop talking nonsense, Shane.'

Shane said to the Professor, 'She doesn't believe me again. Has she always been so dense?'

'I'm not dense at all!' she said indignantly. 'Am I, Father?'

'I believe,' said Will, 'she regards all praise as flattery.'

'And I'm suspicious of flattery. And,' she taunted, smiling, 'flatterers.' Her hand was dropped so suddenly it was almost an insult.

Shane moved towards the door.

'Just a word before you go,' the Professor said. 'How is it you're a truck driver, Shane? Did you change direction when you were within reach of your objective?'

Shane's eyes grew guarded, but Anona spoke instead. 'Educationally he's a moron. He told me so.' Her mouth smiled, but her eyes held a challenge. Shane turned to her sharply, started to speak but stopped.

'Which university, Shane?' Will Willis's question was blunt.

'Only the best,' Anona jeered, 'will do for a truck driver.'

Shane gave her a dismissing look and turned to her father. 'London.' He named the college.

'London, eh?' commented Will.

Anona shook her head in mock sorrow. 'Not Oxford, or Cambridge? Tut, tut!'

Shane's look was so threatening she backed away.

Her father's gaze rested thoughtfully on Shane's face. 'Maybe that's where I've seen you. In my active days I paid occasional visits to that particular college. Subject?'

'Economics.' To Anona, 'Will you see me out?' To her father he extended a hand. 'If you will shake the hand of a deserter from the academic ranks?'

The Professor laughed, their hands meeting briefly. 'Frankly,' said the Professor, head tipped back to meet the younger man's eyes, 'I don't believe that statement.'

Puzzled, Anona looked from one to the other.

At the front door, Shane paused. 'You're nearly there, Miss Willis. If you're not quick, your father may beat you to it.'

'To what?'

'You know the answer to that.' His eyes dwelt musingly on her uplifted face. Had he sensed her longing to hold fast to him, arms around him, cheek against his hard chest? 'A farewell kiss? I think so.'

'No, no, I won't——' Then she was in his arms.

His head lowered slowly, finally claiming his prize. Her arms locked round his neck and her body gave itself to his kiss as if he were about to walk out of her life for ever. When he let her go, he contemplated her bright blue eyes and glowing cheeks, her ruffled hair and moist, inviting lips.

He said softly, 'I'd like to carry you somewhere in my truck as a lucky mascot. You won't begrudge me another, will you, after all that work I've done for you?'

This time his hold was tighter, his lips more audacious. She felt the hardness of the length and breadth of him, the intimate pressure of his thighs against hers, and the crushing of her breasts on his chest as she strained to respond to the urgency of his desire.

Then he was down the garden path to the gate, leaving her deprived and lost and craving for more. Shane bent to speak to Jim who sat in the driving seat of a large car. There was a brief discussion and Shane glanced at his watch. Jim got out and Shane took his place behind the wheel.

Jim made for the cottage, calling, 'Is it possible, miss, for you to take me back to the garage? Mr Shane's late for his appointment and he told me to ask you if you'd mind.'

'Not at all,' Anona replied, and called to her father that she wouldn't be long. As she felt in her purse for the car keys which Jim had given her on his arrival on the doorstep, he turned to the man in the large car and made a thumbs-up sign. Then he put his hand against his temple in a kind of salute.

It was not the kind which would have been exchanged

between colleagues. There was, Anona thought, as she invited Jim to occupy the passenger seat, something slightly deferential in the action.

They talked of general matters and it was not until they were nearing the garage that Anona found the courage to ask the question which had not left her mind since the day her car had broken down.

'Your—your friend,' she said, 'the man called Shane. That man——' her head moved, vaguely indicating the road behind, 'that truck driver who mended my car.'

'Truck driver, miss?' Jim shook his head in amazement. 'He's no truck driver, is Mr Shane.'

'Then—then who is he? What's his other name?'

'Brodie, miss, that's what it is. Mr Shane Brodie. His father's got heart trouble and he's retired. The other son's called Rob. He's younger. So it's Mr Shane Brodie who's in charge now. He's the owner of the business.'

Anona was quiet after her return from the garage. Since her father was watching television, it was not until bedtime that her white face and her quietness came to his notice.

'All evening,' he said as they drank their hot chocolate, 'you haven't been concentrating.' Anona shook her head, but her father insisted, 'You can't fool me, dear. It's an inbuilt sense I have which is left over from my lecturing days. There's something bothering you.'

Anona stared at the dying fire, her hands round her drinking mug. 'That man—Shane.' She spoke jerkily. 'It's Shane *Brodie*.'

'He's one of the family?' The quietness of her father's voice did not disguise the note of horror.

'Not just one of them, he *runs* the haulage company, *manages* it, *controls* it. And,' she burst out, tears near the surface, 'he pretended to be just a truck driver, just an employee. How could he!'

It was then that she realised just how much her emotions

had become involved with the man, how deeply his kisses and his caresses had stirred her. Now that she knew his true identity, they could never again meet on friendly terms.

'We entertained him,' her father said bitterly, 'we invited him into our cottage, we gave him a drink.' Then, with a barely controlled fury, 'I offered him my hand which he held without a qualm!'

He was shaking so much Anona ran over to him, putting her arm around his shoulders. 'You mustn't let it upset you. What good will it do?'

'None.' He was quieter now. Fatigue had tranquillised his mind, calmed his quivering body. But it had not quelled his bitterness. 'And nothing can undo the damage his company, through the carelessness of one of its employees, has done to me.'

Leaving her father, Anona gazed down at the charred logs and wisp of smoke which was all that was left of the fire. 'Nor can anything give us back the money we've lost, or——' Anona half-turned, 'your work at the university.'

'Not to mention my mobility which I miss so sorely that even you, my dear, don't appreciate how much I suffer mentally from its loss.' There was a heavy silence, broken by the settlement of the burned logs into the powdery ash. 'Not a penny in compensation did they pay,' he said in a half-whisper, 'not a letter even, commiserating with me for the injuries they caused.'

'Father,' Anona reminded him gently, 'you admitted in front of witnesses that it was your fault.'

He closed his eyes as if experiencing yet again the anguish and pain the accident had caused him. 'Maybe,' he admitted, sighing. 'I can't bear to think about it any more.'

That night Anona slept fitfully. When she did sleep her dreams were troubled by the face and shape of a man whose shoulders were broad enough to turn the steering

wheel of a giant truck—and bear the burdens of a flourishing business concern. A man whose tough-muscled body
excited, whose lips drew a passionate response, whose
hands could caress—or crush.

Anona was clearing the breakfast dishes when the
telephone rang. Her hand clenched on the receiver as she
said, 'Professor Willis's residence.'

'Anona?' The voice was low-pitched.

Her answer was a stiff, 'Yes?'

After a moment's pause, Shane asked, 'How is your
father today?'

'The same as ever. The same as he always will be.' Her
voice was tense.

She heard his breath, could almost feel it fanning her
cheek. 'I see.' Another silence. 'I want to see you. Are you
free this evening?'

Her anger broke. 'No, *Mr Brodie,* not this evening nor
any other. Not ever as far as you're concerned.'

'So Jim told you.'

'Yes, he did. You kept it a secret, didn't you,' she
accused. 'Why, Mr Brodie? Were you scared, Mr Brodie?
Of me, Mr Brodie? Did you think I might get a knife
and—and slash your tires, bite you and scratch you and
hit you until you——'

'That's enough. You've made your point.'

'No, I haven't.' She was growing hysterical, but she
had to let it all come. 'I haven't even started. You, *your
company,* put my father into a wheelchair for life, took
away his means of livelihood and his freedom of movement. All right, so you denied liability through your
insurance company. But you didn't even pay a penny to
us out of—out of pity—I can't say the kindness of your
heart, because you haven't got one. If I'd known who you
were the other day when you came to my aid, I'd have—
I'd have called the police.' Her heart was beating so fast
she began to feel faint.

More calmly she went on, 'I wish I'd never accepted

the lift you gave me, never l-let you t-touch me, k-kiss me.
I wish I'd never met you!' The tears ran down to her
chin. 'I *hate* you, Mr Brodie, as I've never hated anyone
in my whole life!'

The crash from the other end almost deafened her.

All day Anona worked on her father's book, laboriously
transcribing his difficult handwriting. If hard work held
restorative powers, then she would make sure that, by
unceasing application to her work, she recovered quickly
from the emotional torment into which her brief, if passionate, encounter with Shane Brodie had plunged her.

Work, however, had to be put aside sometimes and it
was during those times—evenings, nights, those long hours
of darkness in her bed—that she found it impossible to
hold her longings at bay. She remembered how angry she
had been when, after many miles on that motorway, it
had dawned on her that the man was deliberately tailing
her. She recalled how he had laughed, throwing back his
head, when he had at last decided to overtake and she had
mouthed her mild curse at him.

Then there was her relief when, having broken down,
she had looked for and seen that scarlet-painted truck
nosing its way towards her, and her relief when he had
braked and climbed down, coming to help her ... So
many other things—secrets she had hugged to herself and
about which she could never tell her father ... Shane's
kisses, the feel of his arms around her.

When, three days later, the letter from Brodie's solicitors arrived, enclosing a letter to which was attached a
cheque for a four-figure sum of money, Will Willis's hand
shook so much the letter fluttered from his fingers. He
turned a dull red.

'Do they think,' he said, 'that *money* will recompense
me for what one of their trucks did to me? Will it give me
back my ability to get up and out of this chair and walk?
Will it allow me to climb down into holes in the earth and

join in the archaeological digs I used to love so much?'

Anona, retrieving the letter read, 'This cheque is sent to you on behalf of my clients, Brodie and Sons, as an *ex gratia* payment, with the intention of helping you financially and, they trust, going some way towards reimbursing you for the money you have lost as a result of your accident. I must emphasise that, in sending you this cheque, my clients are not in any way admitting liability.' The cheque, Anona saw, was signed, 'M. Brodie.'

'It's wonderful!' she exclaimed, staring at the figures on the cheque. 'Now we can buy another car, second-hand, of course——'

'You must return the cheque at once.'

Aghast, Anona said, 'You surely aren't going to let your pride stop you accepting this? We need the money so much, Father. Your book won't be ready for a long time.'

'I'll speed up with my book. We'll spend longer on it each day. I refuse to lower myself to accepting conscience money from that firm, that—that man who came into my house on false pretences. Truck driver, indeed! I should have known. Degree in economics, so obviously a man of culture. He had me fooled, do you hear?'

She had never known her father so angry, and grew worried. 'I'll send it back,' she soothed. 'I'll put it into an envelope and post it right back.'

He shook off her placating hand. 'You'll return it now, Anona. You'll return it, not to the solicitors, but to Brodie's themselves.' His raised hand stopped her protest. 'I want them to understand that I'm throwing their *bribe* back in their faces.'

When Anona entered the red-brick offices which stood an ornamental garden's distance from the road, she wished she was anywhere but where she was. Her father could not possibly know what he had asked of her.

The girl at the desk in the entrance lobby looked up.

'I should like,' said Anona, 'to see Mr Brodie. Mr M. Brodie,' she added, fingering the envelope in her pocket which contained the cheque.

'There are two Mr M. Brodies,' the girl said. 'Mr Morris Brodie and Mr Meredith Brodie.'

Anona thought with an inward smile, How would she react if I said 'Shane'? She said briskly, 'I want to see the man in charge.'

'That would be Mr Meredith Brodie. Have you an appointment?' Anona shook her head. 'Then I'm sorry, but you can't see him without one. I'll contact his secretary and fix a date.'

As the girl dialled, so Anona's heart beat faster. 'I must see him today,' Anona insisted, as the girl waited. She was murmuring, 'Not possible,' when her call was answered.

'I have a lady here,' she said, then looked at Anona. 'I'm sorry—name? A Miss Willis. Says she wants to see Mr Brodie.' The girl listened then looked up. 'When would it be convenient, Miss Willis—the end of this week or next?'

'Now,' said Anona.

'He's at a meeting,' the girl replied blandly.

'Now,' repeated Anona. 'And if Mr Meredith Brodie isn't available, I'll see the man called Shane.'

'Oh.' Into the mouthpiece, the girl murmured, 'She says Shane.' Covering the mouthpiece, she said, 'Mr Brodie's secretary will see what she can do.' The eyes on her were interested.

Ah, Anona thought, her reaction to the name Shane is just like that of the woman at the filling station. 'Yes?' said the girl. 'Er—are you Miss Anona Willis? Yes, she is. Okay. Thanks. Mr Meredith Brodie will see you now, Miss Willis.' She indicated the lift. 'Two floors up, second door on the right.'

Meredith? Anona thought, pressing the button for the lift. Morris? How many 'and Sons' were there connected with the Brodie haulage business? Well, she reflected, stepping in and watching the lift doors glide closed, at least I won't be seeing Shane.

The second door on the right was blank. The third door bore the lettering in white, M. S. Brodie. After a brief knock on the blank door, she opened it to find that the room was unoccupied. Unaccountably this annoyed her. It was not that she had expected a welcoming party, but an empty room constituted an affront.

The communicating door to her left was closed. It was a barrier and it was a challenge. It counteracted the great reluctance she had felt in carrying out her father's wishes and returning by hand the money Brodie's had so belatedly offered.

While the hackles of her temper were rising, she walked to the door and opened it. If Mr Meredith Brodie proved to be as unpleasant as the actions of his company after her father's accident had implied, then that cheque would be crushed into a ball and hurled at his despotic face.

'Mr Meredith Brodie?' she was saying, holding on to the door handle—then she saw the man behind the desk.

CHAPTER FIVE

FOR an instant her eyes locked with his. Only a few days had passed since she had seen him, yet the gulf of time, status and circumstance which now separated them seemed unbridgeable.

Her heart throbbed like a jungle drum, her breaths came quickly. 'What are you doing here?' she asked, watching dazedly as Shane Brodie rose in greeting.

'I might ask the same of you.' His eyes were cool, his manner remote.

'I was told I'd see a Mr Meredith Brodie. You're not——' On the other door had been the name M. S. Brodie. 'Are you?' She took the envelope from her pocket, extracting the cheque. 'Was it you who signed this?'

'The signature's mine. Why?' He lowered himself to his chair, inviting her silently to occupy the other chair. She remained standing.

'Why? *Why?*' Now she was her father's emissary, taking on his anger, his outrage, even using his words. 'Did you really think,' she said 'that *money* could recompense my father for what one of your drivers did to him? Did you think it would give him back the use of his legs? Allow him to join in archaeological digs as he used to do— it was his greatest joy—and give advice and encouragement to his students in their efforts?'

Shane leaned back in his chair and watched her impassively.

'My father called it conscience money,' she went on, her voice rising, 'and he was right. You saw him for the first time the other day, when you came to our cottage. You saw just what a low state your company had reduced him to. My father in a wheelchair, my father dependent

63

on another person for all his needs with no hope of a cure.'

Her eyes were moistening, but she would not weaken in front of him. He had picked up a pen and was drawing outlines on an envelope. The very action revealed his unconcern, she thought angrily.

'He used to be such a fine man,' she went on, 'tall, commanding. Intellectually he was far ahead of others in his own line. He was respected throughout the university, consulted as an authority on his subject by newspapers and learned journals. Now look at him!' Her voice broke. 'Living half-forgotten in a tiny cottage in academic exile.'

Her legs felt weak and she sought the chair she had first refused.

Shane threw down the pen, sitting upright and pulling on his jacket which emphasised the breadth of his shoulders. A picture flashed before her of his body as she had first seen it and she remembered the toughness of him, the strength of his arms as they manipulated the wheel of the truck—or manipulated her emotions and her body so as to extract from her the greatest response.

'There's something you've overlooked,' he said at last. 'The accident was due to your father's carelessness, not our company's.'

'And there's something you've overlooked,' she crumpled the cheque, 'that money can't buy back health and mobility that are lost for ever.' The crushed cheque was withdrawn from her pocket and hurled towards him, at his face as her father had directed. It hit him just below the eye, then dropped to the floor.

He was pushing back his chair, moving round the desk and grasping her wrists before she could utter a word of apology. 'My father,' she muttered, wincing with the pain, 'he told me to throw your bribe back in your face.'

He twisted an arm behind her and dragged her towards him. His jaw was rigid, thrust forward while his eyes burned down into hers. 'You little vixen,' he rasped, 'you ungrateful little bitch, I'll——'

'I told you,' she cried, 'it wasn't my idea. I carried out my father's orders. Please,' her lip quivered, 'you're hurting me. I can't stand it.' He was unmoved. 'If you put my arm out of action,' she whispered, 'I won't be able to type my father's script and that will delay its completion even more. Please ...'

Slowly, reluctantly, his hold was relaxed and relief momentarily blotted out pain. But as the blood flowed back, the pain in her left arm caught up with her. With her right hand she massaged it, but the ache persisted. There was an ache somewhere else, too. It was impossible to pinpoint the exact place, but the tears she had endeavoured to suppress welled over. A sob escaped her and she swung away, saying, 'I'm sorry, I'm taking up your time.'

Footsteps sounded behind her and she thought, He's going to show me out. I'll go before he—— Two strong hands settled on her shoulders, two thumbs rubbed gently. A hand slid down her right arm, finding her hand.

'Come with me.' He pulled her behind him towards the communicating door, opening it. 'Jenny,' he said, 'I'll be out for about an hour. When I get back I'd like to have a chat with my father.' He closed the door and led Anona to the main entrance door. It swung open and there was 'M. S. Brodie' again. Meredith Shane ... Meredith Shane Brodie. Was Morris Brodie his father?

'Where are we going?' she demanded.

'You'll see soon enough.'

He took her to the rear of the building. His car was parked in a reserved place and he unlocked it, putting her into the car and himself into the driving seat. He reversed and, with a muted roar, the car drove forward to join the main road.

It was not long before the car turned off the busy road into a quieter, less used side road. A short distance on, he

turned right yet again and before them rose the emerald
green of the north Derbyshire moorland stretching in wild
grandeur to the grey-blue sky.

In the near-distance was the imposing height of Mam
Tor which, Anona remembered her father telling her, was
known as the 'Shivering Mountain' because of constantly
recurring landslides. These were caused, he had said,
by the strange composition of shale and grit in alternate
layers, a fact which had been noted as far back as in
Elizabethan times.

Shane edged the car off the road and on to the uneven
grass. As the noise of the engine died so the awesome
silence took over, invading the car through the opened
windows. It intruded upon the thoughts through the eyes
and ears, invading the body through the breathed-in
freshness of the windswept air.

The beauty all around her, however, did more to increase rather than diminish Anona's dilemma. She could
not find it in her to give it the attention and admiration
it demanded.

'Why,' she asked Shane, 'have you brought me here?'

'We can talk,' he looked around, 'away from pressures,
in calmness, among the tranquillity of the hills.'

Anona followed the movement of the clock on the
dashboard, leant forward and turned the radio on and off.
He watched her as if she were a child trying out a new
toy. 'Talk about what?' she asked at last.

'The money you threw back at me.'

'On my father's orders.'

'If you'd had your way you would have accepted it?'

She thought about the answer. If she said 'yes', what
reason could she give to substantiate her answer? Her
father had at the time of the accident admitted to being
in the wrong, which meant that Brodie's insurance company had rightly denied their client's responsibility.

With a sigh she gazed at the landscape, now flooded

with gold as the sun broke through, now darkly brooding as the clouds had their way. When she spoke, her voice was strained. 'The money would have been useful. I told my father so, but he wouldn't listen.' A short silence followed as she watched two white birds swoop and fly on, one in pursuit of the other. 'I need another car. The one I have won't last much longer. As you know, of course.'

'Which means that the money I offered would have gone a long way to solving your problems. Yet you won't accept.'

'I *can't* accept it. One thing I won't do is go against my father's wishes. He's suffered enough without having his daughter trying to put pressure on him, no matter what the reason.'

She reached for the door catch and stepped out on to the soft moorland turf. Her eyes roamed over mountain and moors, finding a village nestling in a hollow, its cottages built with grey stone and red-slated roofs. There were the barns and rambling buildings of a handful of farms, the scattering of trees and sprawling bushes in full leaf both sheltering and drawing attention to the small patch of human life and warmth amongst the daunting wild terrain around them.

'Anona.' Shane had come to her side and was pulling her to him, his arm tightly about her waist. 'I fancy another taste of honey from those lips of yours.' An eyebrow lifted. 'Any objections?' He gave her no chance to answer.

His mouth was on to hers, touching, lifting, teasing, tormenting, moving from centre to corner until, with a half-angry cry, she lifted her arms and crossed them at his neck, holding him still and returning all his kisses in one.

Breaking away, she stared up at him, alarmed at her own action. She had taken the initiative, wordlessly told him, 'I can't hold out against you, I find you irresistible.' Yes, he'd heard her silent message. His eyes burned into hers, his lips curved with a mixture of delight and victory. His arms urged her to him and he eased her down on to the velvet-feel of the green moorland grass.

The ground sloped away from the roadside and he rolled her over and over until they reached a level piece of land, out of sight of any vehicle that might go by. The abandoned clinging and moving together of their two bodies had stimulated and excited, bringing a laughing brightness to her eyes and a wide, inviting smile to her moist lips.

His head lifted although his arms around her were tight as steel bands. He gazed into her face and she saw his features through a haze—the etched lines from cheek to chin, the jutting jaw, the thick brows almost meeting. His hair was wind-blown, the suit he wore stretched tautly across his broad back.

'Your jacket,' she said, 'there's pieces of grass on it.'

'And there are twigs in your hair and sunbeams in your eyes.'

'You shouldn't be here. It's in the middle of your working day.'

'What if it is? I'm the boss.'

The boss, the head of the business, a company called Brodie's ... And Brodie's had taken away from her father most of the things that made life worth living.

'Now what are you thinking, my pet? Cloud shadows have taken the place of the sunbeams in those eyes of yours. I'll put them back, like this, and this.'

He rained kisses over her face, finishing with the tip of her nose. Her eyes squeezed shut in mock annoyance and he laughed and swooped to capture her lips. Her hands slipped inside his jacket and she felt beneath her outspread fingers the ridges of his shoulder blades and the firm muscles below them. His hands were also on a voyage of discovery over her tingling body and she was conscious of his masculine desires, his male dominance to which she craved to yield.

When his mouth lifted at last, freeing hers, she whispered, 'Shane, Shane ...' If only she could surrender here, now, merging with him as one. 'My father—he'll be wondering where I am, what I'm doing '

Hard fingers pinched her chin. 'And are you going to tell him what you've been doing?' His smile gently mocked, his eyes roved over her face, touching down on brow and eye and lips.

His question was like a long shadow over the golden morning. 'He's bitter, Shane,' she said, running her finger through the cleft in his chin. 'He's angry, about the cheque, about the way——' She tried to ease him from her, but it was like trying to move a truck with her two bare hands.

He stayed where he was. 'About the way——?'

'The way he——' Her head moved to one side and she glimpsed the formidable line of the surrounding hills. If she told him, he would draw away in mind and body. The fingers caught again at her chin, forcing an answer. 'The way he entertained a—a member of the Brodie family without knowing it. He can't forgive them for what their company has done to him.'

Shane moved away, resting on a hand and elbow, gazing narrow-eyed at the green and gold hills. He had gone from her and she clamoured inside for his return, but he had retreated into a harsher world than the one which in those precious moments had enfolded them.

'He's too proud to take money.'

'Too stubborn, shouldn't you have said? How long does he intend blaming us for what was really his fault?' It was a question she could not answer. 'You need the money— you told me. Is there no way in which he can be persuaded——'

'None, Shane. He called it conscience money.' Shane's long legs moved irritably. 'He told me to throw it back in your face.'

He twisted back to her, rolling over, imprisoning her again. 'Which you did, you imp. Shall I spank you for it?'

He jerked her on to her front and brought his hand down, none too gently, once, twice, on to her rear.

Indignantly, face flushed, Anona escaped his hold and rolled from him, rising and brushing herself. He got up slowly and confronted her and she saw twin sparks of fire in his eyes. His arms thrust towards her, but another kiss would be her undoing. Turning, she ran, breathing hard, up the slope to the road, reaching the car and holding on to it as if it were a sanctuary from him. Passing traffic saved her and she pointed, laughing, at the vehicles which approached at intervals along the road which wound back into the distance.

'Lucky for you, my girl,' he said. 'Otherwise ...' His swift up-and-down scrutiny of her shapeliness revealed clearly the thoughts that were in his mind.

Driving back she said, 'There's grass and bits still on your jacket. What will people think if the managing director arrives at his office as if he'd——'

'Been tumbling a girl in the grass,' he finished, with a broad, reflective smile. 'They'd think I was human after all! Come on, brush all the evidence away.'

Laughing, she reached up and picked pieces from his hair and ran a hand lightly down his sleeve and across his shoulders. Her hand wanted to linger on his back, enjoying the feeling that, in the light of their recent closer intimacy, she could touch him at will.

He shot her a glance and smiled. It was as if he had guessed her thoughts. 'When can we meet again?'

The question made her feel inside as unstable and crumbling as Mam Tor.

'I can't answer that,' she answered numbly.

After a silence, Shane said, 'Do I take it that you would like to but you don't want to go against your father?'

'It's impossible for me to go against him,' she said quietly. 'He depends on me so much.'

They were nearing her home now. 'So,' said Shane, 'no money and no meeting. Is that how you want it?'

She could not be disloyal to her father again. Shane drew up a few cottages distant and Anona thanked him silently for his discretion. After all this time he probably guessed that her father would be looking out for her. She tensed for a lie. 'It's how I want it.'

'Okay.' There was a hard note to his voice. 'That's how it shall be. Are you getting out?'

His cold curtness had her colouring. He could not wait to be rid of her presence, in spite of those golden moments in the shadow of the Shivering Mountain. Yet there she was, lingering as if waiting for his goodbye kiss.

Slamming the door shut, she bent and said, 'Thanks for the outing. I—enjoyed the—break.'

He hit back, 'Thank *you* for the romantic interlude. I enjoyed the *break,* too.'

Recognising the double meaning, she compressed her lips and gazed expressionessly back at him. As he drove away, it was as if her heart was shifting and shivering like Mam Tor.

It was towards the end of the following week that a red van drew up outside the cottage. It bore the name of Brodie.

Anona was standing at the front window staring out. Her thoughts, as they so often were, had been with the man whose substance she had held in her arms, yet now seemed to have turned into a shadow. When his surname materialised before her eyes, it brought her instantly to life. Who but Shane would call on them? She knew no other Brodie.

The man at the wheel she recognised as Jim. The passenger, who was easing himself from the front seat, was a stranger to her. Yet there was something about his face that held a likeness to—someone she knew.

As the visitor straightened to his full height, which was lessened only slightly by stooping shoulders, Anona saw his greying hair and weather-toughened face. The man was an older version of Shane Brodie. His arms hung loosely, his eyes roamed over the modest dwelling, seeing suddenly the face of a girl looking out. He bent to speak to Jim and the van moved on.

A Brodie, Anona thought, another Brodie seeking entry to their cottage? She glanced at her father, absorbed in a book. Would he turn the man away—a man of his own generation?

The visitor was smiling now, walking slowly from the gate he had carefully closed behind him. He wore a bright-eyed look of anticipated welcome.

'Father,' Anona said urgently, making him lift his head from his book, 'there's a man coming here, a stranger.'

'What man?' Will Willis's brow pleated. 'Kenny Patterson from next door? Let him in——'

'A stranger, Father,' she repeated gently.

He put his book aside, seeming pleased. 'Strangers are welcome in this cottage. I've never yet turned away a stranger from my door.'

Anona went into the entrance hall as the knock sounded. The man stood on the doorstep, still smiling, and she had to lift her head to look at the man. There were deep lines etched into his cheeks, laughter lines raying out from his eyes, thick, greying eyebrows. 'Miss Willis?' His voice was deep and bore the accent of the area in which he had probably lived all his life. 'My name's Brodie, Morris Brodie.' He rubbed his hands together, looking a little awkward.

Anona's hand came out, firm and almost defiant. 'Welcome to our house, Mr Brodie.' She had spoken loudly for her father's benefit. 'Please come in.'

'Brodie?' Her father's voice came sharply from the living-room. 'I'll have no Brodie again in my cottage! Tell him to get out. Last time he came he fooled me into offering my hand in friendship. Show him the door, Anona.'

Dismayed, Anona whispered, 'Please wait a moment, Mr Brodie.' She went into the living-room, confronting her father. 'You said you'd never turn away a stranger. I told you, Father,' she lowered her voice, 'it's an older man, not the one——.'

'Mr Willis?' The man was in the room, looking with a kind of diffident gentleness at the man in the wheelchair. 'If you don't want me here, I'll go. I'd never push my way unwanted into anyone's house, especially yours.'

Disarmed by the visitor's candid approach, Will Willis looked into the fading brown eyes of the senior Brodie. He could not have missed the diffidence and the gentleness which was interwoven with the undoubted pride implicit in the man's bearing. A shaft of light must have exposed a deep-buried relic of forgiveness in Will's brain.

'You're welcome to stay,' he said gruffly. Anona knew how much it must have cost him to utter those words to a member of the Brodie family.

'A drink?' Anona asked, happily.

'No alcohol for me,' their visitor declined. 'Never touched it in my truck driving days, nor do I now.' He gestured towards his chest. 'This old heart of mine's giving me a bit of trouble and I have to go carefully. Now a nice cup of tea——?'

'Of course. Father?' He nodded.

Will's pallor was receding. The wrath which had chilled his keen eyes had given way to a wary toleration of the stranger who, like his younger namesake—his son?—seemed to dominate the room.

While Anona prepared the pot of tea, there was a sound of talking from the living-room. The silence she had dreaded had not occurred. As she carried in the tray Morris Brodie was saying,

'Yes, we're a self-made family, Mr Willis.' Her father did not appear to resent the omission of his courtesy title. 'My father's father—last century, that was—started it all with a horse and cart. My father took the business over. By then things were being mechanised, not least the first load-carriers.' He nodded his thanks as Anona handed him tea and sugar. This he heaped into his cup.

'That was after the steam wagons?' Will Willis asked, refusing the sugar.

Morris Brodie was nodding vigorously. 'And it's changed again. My, how it's changed! But one tradition lives on—the one of passing the business on from father to son, two sons in my case. There's Shane,' he turned to an interested Anona, 'you know him. He's boss now. I had to retire,' he indicated his chest, 'but I knew he'd do the company good. Knows it all backwards, does Shane, from Z to A. Fine lad. And there's Rob.'

Anona remembered the name at once. So it had been his brother to whom Shane had spoken that day her car had broken down.

'I gave 'em both a good education—another family tradition, one I made.' He laughed at himself. 'Shane came through it best. Even at school he was top in everything. But Rob never was one for lessons and learning. Rob's got himself a wife, I'm still waiting for Shane to find the right girl. They've come and gone in his life.' Morris gladly accepted a second cup of tea. 'Can't find one he wants to keep, though! Or so he says.' The visitor laughed again, loudly, then drank in large swallows and put down his empty cup.

Will Willis smiled. 'Is your company still expanding?' he asked.

'My son wouldn't have it otherwise.' Morris folded his long arms, arms which, in their day, must like his son have steered fully-loaded trucks over many miles of road and highway. His suit, creased and shiny with age, had surely been worn especially for the visit. The gesture touched Anona's heart. It spoke, not of the need to impress—there was nothing of that about this man—but of a desire to convey a feeling of respect towards his host.

'Shane said you were determined to remain independent,' Anona ventured. She remembered how Shane had shown unexpected loyalty—as she had then regarded it—

towards his firm, speaking with pride of how they had resisted takeover bids.

Morris nodded vigorously. 'We've had offers, plenty of 'em, but what's Brodie's stays Brodie's. It's a family motto,' he explained proudly. 'We've got about twenty vehicles, some of them heavy rigids, that is, sixteen and eighteen-ton trucks, and some of them thirty-two-ton trucks.'

'You carry containers?' Will asked, losing his reserve at last in his interest in his guest's conversation.

Morris Brodie nodded, 'And TIR trailers.'

'I've often wondered,' said Anona, 'what those letters stand for.'

'Ah, yes,' their guest responded, his face flushing with the pleasure of talking about the subject nearest to his heart. 'It means Transports Internationales Routiers. Vehicles with those letters on them can be Customs-sealed at the start of their journey and carry on to a foreign destination without having to be inspected at the frontiers. Very useful, that,' he added.

It was then that he seemed to recall why he had come. A long arm lifted to rub the back of his head. Two long legs stretched out and crossed, not easily as in relaxation but taut with tension. A foot twisted this way and that. Anona offered him a biscuit, which he declined.

'Takes a lot of running, does Brodie's,' he observed, watching his moving foot as if it were not part of him. 'My son Shane holds the purse-strings and,' with a smile, 'all the other strings, too. My son Rob runs the garage.'

'Where my car was repaired?' Anona enquired.

Morris nodded. 'You were honoured, you know, in getting my son Shane to mend your car. It's not often he'd do such a thing for a stranger. He must have taken a fancy to you!'

Anona coloured and laughed, hugging to herself the secret of just how close her relationship with his son had become.

Will found Morris's remark amusing, saying, to his daughter's astonishment, 'And why not? She's a good-looking girl, with brains.'

'You're right, Mr Willis. You're right to be proud of her. I expect she's got a string of young lads after her.' He did not wait for confirmation or denial of the statement. 'You're a widower, aren't you?' he asked. 'Like me. I miss the wife.' He stared sadly at his twisting feet. 'She was good to me and for me.' He sighed. 'Elsa, Rob's wife, manages the office. My nephew, Spencer, runs the traffic side of the business, taking instructions from customers and so on.'

'It sounds,' said Will, 'far more complicated a matter organising a haulage business than I ever dreamed.'

Anona thought, with a leap of hope, He's becoming reconciled to Brodie's at last. If I met Shane sometimes, as he asked me to do, would Father object now, or would he——? Then she remembered that a week had passed since she had seen Shane. He had made no effort to continue their acquaintance.

'It was the filling station we own I came to see you about,' Morris was saying. 'The pumps are self-service and the man we employ to take the money is off work. Albert's around seventy, but there's plenty of life in him yet. The trouble is he suffers from back trouble. Rob runs the repair workshop, plus the filling station.'

'I know they're both on the same site,' Anona put in.

Morris nodded. 'But Rob can't be everywhere at once, which means he can't spare the time to sit in the shop taking the money, too. So we were wondering——' his eyes wandered cautiously to Anona then back to her father, 'if you, Professor——'

Anona thought, My father's courtesy title at last, the delicate flattery, the trump card—Morris Brodie's no fool.

'If you,' Morris went on, 'could spare your clever daughter to help us out at the filling station shop while old Albert's away.'

This, Anona was certain, was another way that Brodie's boss had thought up of getting around her father's deep-seated prejudice against them, against his refusal to accept from them any financial help. Would her father see the offer for what it was, or would he be taken in by its subtlety?

Will Willis's face was flushed, but not with anger, Anona saw with relief. His colour was heightened by the effect of the absorbing conversation he had had with his visitor. The differences in status and social standing had melted away. Morris Brodie had proved himself to be an interesting man. This was all that had mattered.

'Of course I could spare my daughter,' Will replied, 'as long as the arrangement is temporary. Provided she's willing.' He smiled at Anona. He had been completely taken in by Morris's subtle, yet honest, approach.

'But your book,' she reminded him gently.

'No hurry for that, is there?'

Anona, handling the dwindling family finances, knew differently, but she did not remonstrate. The prospect of going out to work again, mixing with others, was too inviting to be lightly cast aside.

'We'd pay you, of course,' said Morris. 'A good rate per hour. Us Brodies aren't mean with our money ...' He stopped, glancing uncomfortably from daughter to father. The return of the cheque ... he had just remembered. If his words had been taken wrongly, his whole case could have been undermined.

'And,' Anona intervened swiftly, hoping to defuse any explosive situation arising from the unguarded statement, 'we Willises aren't beggars, Mr Brodie. We're proud, too.' Her father nodded.

'I'm glad to hear it,' said Morris, lifting his considerable length from the chair. 'Every family should have its pride. And loyalty.'

'And love,' Anona finished, smiling.

'Most certainly love,' agreed Morris.

Will seemed to appreciate the firm handclasp, the warmth of the big man reaching out to him. 'Come again, Morris,' he said. 'And it's Will, not Mister.'

'Will it will be,' joked Morris. 'And I'll come again for sure.' To Anona, 'I should have asked, will you help us out?' She nodded eagerly. 'Would tomorrow suit? Our day starts at six o'clock in the morning,' Anona's eyes opened wide, 'but we wouldn't expect you till half nine.'

Anona confirmed, 'I'll be there.'

'Fine.' At the door he turned. 'Will—is it short for William?'

Professor Willis laughed. 'I wish it were. It's Willis Willis. You see, I had parents with a bit too much sense of humour!'

Morris Brodie laughed loudly and was still chuckling as he made for the garden gate and the small red van which had appeared from nowhere.

CHAPTER SIX

It was almost half-past nine when Anona steered her car into a parking place at the side of the filling station. The Pattersons next door had agreed to look after her father, giving him his midday meal.

It was a little unnerving to be working away from home again. In view of the nature of the job, she had decided to wear slacks and a check shirt instead of a dress. The day was warm and cars had formed a line and their drivers waited patiently for their turn at the petrol pumps. The sunshine, it seemed, had already enticed the tourists from their camping grounds or hotels.

The glass door clicked and Anona remembered the last time she had been in that shop. A young woman had sat behind the counter taking money. When she heard the name 'Shane' she had stared, and no wonder, Anona thought. Calling the owner of the business by one of his forenames must have placed her very firmly, in the young woman's mind, in a certain special category.

This time the chair was occupied by a man in his late twenties. He was dark-haired, tall and had the unmistakable Brodie look. On his white shirt the name Brodie was, as usual, embroidered in red.

As Anona entered, the man looked up. On his face was an expression of irritability rather than welcome. He seemed to know that she was not just another customer. Maybe, she thought, a detailed description of her had been passed round the family!

'Mr Brodie?' she asked. He was almost as good-looking as his elder brother, but without that brother's physique or strength of character.

'Rob Brodie,' he said, rising. 'I'm glad you've come at

79

last. We've been open since eight this morning and I've been on my own trying to cope. You are Miss Willis, aren't you? Thank heaven for that. Put your things down somewhere,' he looked vaguely around, 'and I'll give you a quick lesson in how to operate this till.'

'I'll do that. You carry on serving the customers.'

Anona looked up, her heart bumping unevenly. How had Shane entered without their hearing him? Of course, there must be a rear entrance, probably from the café. From the chair she was occupying, she gazed into his face. How many days had passed since she had seen him? Years, wasn't it? she thought feverishly.

The words he had spoken when they had parted came back to her. 'Thank you for the romantic interlude.' That was all it had been, from the moment she had met him—an interlude. It was something she must remember, no matter how many times she might see him while she worked for Brodie's.

He, too, wore a Brodie shirt. His jeans were creased and oil-smeared. Out of one pocket bulged a spanner. Boss or no boss, he was here to work. He bent over her, one hand on the counter, the other on the back of her chair. He gave her a quick, lopsided smile. It set her heart skipping again and brought an answering smile to her mouth.

Rob, who had no chance to object to being given orders on his own territory, moved away. Since he had been staring unpleasantly at his brother, he must have seen the silent, slightly intimate exchange.

A customer entered and paid for his purchase by credit card. Shane was able to explain to Anona how such cards were dealt with. Another paid with cash and this Shane demonstrated, too. Yet another customer wished to pay by cheque and it was not long before Anona understood how to deal with the automated method of accepting payment.

When the teaching session had ended, Anona felt a stab of disappointment. Shane no longer stood close. His strong arms, rough with dark hair, no longer supported him or brushed her arms as they moved to indicate a point she had overlooked.

While the customers came in, Shane stood nearby watching Anona deal with each person. After about twenty minutes, he seemed satisfied that she could cope with the situation and prepared to leave. There was a pause in the demand for her services and he stood on the customers' side of the counter, looking down at her.

'I hear your father accepted the suggestion that you might come and help us without a single objection.'

'I was as surprised as you. I think your father charmed him into acting out of character. He's——' she fiddled with a pencil, 'he's quite a personality, your father.'

He took the spanner from his pocket and tapped it against his palm. 'I'm glad you liked him.' A frown passed across his face. 'He's not in full health.'

Rob left the shop, saying he'd be back in a couple of minutes.

Anona nodded and said to Shane, 'You seem to be fond of your father.'

'Yes.' He said no more on the subject. 'How do you feel about being a real live working girl again?'

'It feels great. It can get a bit—well, claustrophobic living and working at home. I'd begun to miss the company of people my age. So,' her blue eyes and shy smile lifted to his, 'thanks for what you've done.'

Shane smiled back. 'I don't know why I bothered. You're the first girl to turn down the chance of a date with me.'

Rob came back noisily, looking with irritation at his brother's back. 'You still here?' Shane did not respond. 'Beware of my big brother, Miss Willis. It's his line, chatting up all the female talent in sight.'

The spanner tapped harder against Shane's palm.

'He's a wolf, Miss Willis,' Rob persisted, 'a wolf in a crawling mechanic's clothing.'

Dismayed at the younger brother's goading, Anona

glanced at Shane. She had not missed the underlying meaning. Nor had Shane, judging by the hardening of his jawline.

'Or,' Rob added, 'his Savile Row suit, depending on whichever part he's playing at the time of the pursuit.'

A customer's entrance put an end to the one-sided quarrel. As Anona dealt with the exchange of money, Shane went out, the spanner bulging in his pocket again.

At noon, Rob informed her that she had an hour for lunch. When she returned, he told her, he would go for his meal. He described where the self-service café was situated, but she said that she already knew. He looked puzzled at this, then shrugged.

Choosing a seat by the café window, Anona ate the meat salad she had carried from the service counter. Looking out, she watched Brodie vehicles arriving and leaving. Being so large they were driven with care over the uneven ground. One of the trucks reminded her of the one in which she had been given a lift by the arrogant, laughing truck driver that hot day not so long ago.

Even when she had been seated high in his cab, he had puzzled her by his good speaking voice and his possession of an intellect which seemed to be well above that required of an average truck driver. A drop-out, he'd called himself!

When the man entered the café, her knife dropped to the table. Confused, she retrieved it, hoping to have escaped unnoticed, but he had seen her. Paying for the contents of his tray, he left the girl at the cash desk laughing at his joke. Anona tried in vain to pretend she was invisible.

'No sand to bury your head in,' said a familiar voice, 'so you use the food on your plate instead.' A chair scraped, the table juddered as he seated himself. 'Was it a case of "Think of the devil and——"'

'Yes.' She raised her head, looking at him, seeing his grease-stained shirt, the way it hung loose and partly buttoned, at his gold watch and the way it fastened down the hairs around his wrist.

He sorted out his meal. He, too, had chosen a salad. On that journey along the motorway, Anona remembered how he had said, on offering her his sandwiches, 'I make a point of never over-eating.' From the meagre meal he had selected, it seemed it was a resolution to which he adhered. He asked with a faint smile, 'Were they good thoughts or bad?'

'Both,' she answered with a quick grin. 'I remembered how that day you gave me a lift you called yourself a drop-out. Some drop-out—boss of a thriving haulage business and owning one of the most expensive sports cars on the market!' He listened with a bland smile as she pursued her theme. 'With the ability to turn into an executive or a repairer of cars at the flick of a switch inside your super-intelligent brain.'

He bowed over his grated carrot and sliced tomato. 'Thank you, ma'am. Next time I need a reference, ma'am, I'll give your name——' his eyebrows lifted in mock-earnestness, 'that is, ma'am, if you'll give me your kind permission?' Then his eyes crinkled and her heart bounded. 'But it's not only cars I can repair, it's trucks, too. There isn't one that our family owns I couldn't, if necessary, get into or under and put right.'

He saw her surprise and went on, 'In most family firms like ours, the sons are expected to take over one day. So as soon as they're old enough, they're taught every aspect of the job, starting at the bottom—literally at ground level—and working through every stage. Which is how I can drive trucks as well as manage the firm.'

'What about your brother? He doesn't seem so keen, so—well, gifted as you or as enthusiastic.'

'So you've noticed? You're a perceptive creature for a woman—ah,' he put out a hand to cover hers which had rolled her paper napkin into a ball preparatory to throwing it, 'you're eating with the boss, so behave!'

The women at the counter were staring and Anona coloured deeply. 'Sorry,' she mumbled. 'Half the world and his wife—especially his wife—are looking at us.'

'And no wonder. It's not many employees who would threaten to throw something at the head of the firm.'

Anona looked suitably abashed, but could not suppress a smile as she rose to leave. 'Please excuse me, Mr Brodie,' her smile turned provocative. 'I shall be late back and that just wouldn't do on my first day, would it, even if it is the boss who's keeping me!'

He half-rose out of politeness and said, 'Will you come out with me tonight?'

A frown dulled her eyes. 'I thought I told you my father wouldn't like——'

'Forget I asked.' He turned his attention entirely to his meal.

Her father was alone when she arrived home from work. To Anona's relief, he was deep in his work. She had visualised an anxious face watching for her, but it seemed the anxiety had been all on her part.

'Plenty of work for me?' she asked lightly.

'Not too much,' was his reply. 'I became absorbed in the research and,' with a smile, 'you know that's fatal for my output of words. Well,' with a sigh as the tension of hours of absorption in his subject fell from him, 'how did my daughter fare on her first day's work for nearly two years outside the home?'

'I enjoyed it, even though it was only taking money from customers and not even having to use my brain adding up or taking away. There was a machine to do it all.'

'Highly automated?' Will asked. As she nodded, he tutted as if condemning all those responsible for imposing electronics and technology on to mankind. He returned to his work.

'Cup of tea, Father?' He replied that that would be very nice. He'd had a good lunch, he called to her as she went into the kitchen. They drank their tea in companionable silence.

While her father worked, Anona thought about Shane's invitation and wished she had accepted. An invitation to go out with him meant exactly that. It implied nothing more than friendship and certainly no emotional involvement. Then the thought came—was it friendship she wanted? Wasn't involvement with such a man something to be desired, to accept with both hands if it were offered?

The time ten days or so ago when they had rolled down the bank together formed a picture in her mind. It was as if she were thinking about another couple, an episode in two other people's lives. She remembered Shane's kisses, the strength of his arms, the way her heart sang like the larks rising over the surrounding moors.

With a sigh she rose and gathered the cups, washing and drying them automatically, feeling the time hang and wishing her work with Brodie's was full-time, and had not ended when the clock reached three.

The evening meal had been cleared and Anona stared out at the sun-filled evening. Even though it was full of golden summer sounds, to her it was empty. When a sprawling pale blue car slowed to a stop outside, she could not believe her eyes. When the tall, confident, striding figure approached the front door, she ran to open it, making no attempt to hide her eagerness.

Only with words did she try to push him away. 'I told you no,' she said, eyes bright, smile flickering, 'I wouldn't go out with you because——'

His fingers rested against her lips. 'You told me neither yes nor no, only that your father——'

With a hasty movement she indicated that her father could hear them. In mime he asked if he could come in. She mouthed, 'I'm sorry,' and stood back, letting him enter.

He went with confident footsteps to the living-room. Alarmed, she hoped her father would contain his anger at the intrusion. Swiftly she followed and heard Shane say,

'Good evening, Professor Willis.' He spoke briskly.

'Good evening, Mr Brodie.' The reply was studiedly formal. At the tone, Anona's heart sank. She knew her father's moods and this was Professor Willis Willis at his most unbending.

Anona came to a stop beside Shane. 'I've come,' said Shane to his reluctant host, 'to ask your permission to borrow your daughter.'

The Professor's pain-shadowed eyes met the unflinching grey ones above him, but Will's voice was as robust as his body once was. 'For what purpose, may I ask?'

'Companionship, an evening drive.' A pause, then, 'My intentions are strictly honourable.'

The Professor gave the faintest wince. Had he caught a glimpse of a lonely future? Had the realisation that he could not for ever hope to hold on to his daughter filled him with dread?

His head turned slowly. 'Anona?' Even before she could respond, her father had read in her eyes all he needed to know. To Shane he said, 'How long will this evening drive take?'

Shane looked at Anona and a flicker of something passed across his eyes. Was it a private rejoicing at his own success? 'Your question.'

Flustered by Shane's tactics, Anona said, 'An hour? Two hours? I just don't know. It's Shane's idea, not mine.'

A soundless sigh expanded and contracted Will's lungs. It was as if he were capitulating in the face of something which he had long accepted would never be his again—youth, mobility, the joy of living.

'If you want to go, Anona,' he said at last, 'please feel free to do so.'

'Thanks, Father,' Anona answered, smothering the impulse to throw her arms around his neck.

'Get a jacket or something,' Shane told her, and she nodded, hurrying into the entrance lobby. For a moment Shane stood looking down at the bent and greying head. If there was compassion in the younger man's eyes, the Professor did not see it. 'Thank you, Professor Willis,' Shane said at last.

The bowed head was lifted. 'For what, Mr Brodie? For my daughter's company? It's worth having, I can tell you that. To me it's priceless.'

Anona, having heard the exchange, stood watching in the doorway. Had her father's words been spoken out of possessiveness or warning?

'A couple of hours, Father,' she promised, 'that's all.'

'Enjoy your drive,' Will remarked. After a short pause he added, 'Both of you.'

The evening sun threw the shadows of the hill-clinging trees and shrubs down the steep slopes which rose in a green line all around them.

Anona still could not believe that she sat beside the man who, from the moment of their meeting, had occupied her thoughts. 'Why did you come for me?' she asked. 'You still haven't explained.'

Did she really want an explanation? Wasn't it enough that they were there, together? That, in itself, was like a dream and only a fool tore a dream apart to discover what it was made of ...

'You told me your father wouldn't like it,' he stated. 'It was a challenge I couldn't resist.'

So cold reason had prompted his action, nothing more. Well—she sighed and stared at the passing scenery—she had been the fool. She had torn her dream apart and found that it was made of candyfloss which melted in her hand.

'Your theory didn't stand up to the test,' he was saying.

His quick taunting glance had her heartbeats spinning with the wheels. 'I have a theory, too. That all barriers—within reason—are built to be broken.'

They were passing through Baslow, with its ancient three-arched bridge spanning the river Derwent. A mist was forming, softening the hills and adding mystery to their beauty. Shane turned sharply right and it was not long before the great and famous house of Chatsworth came into view.

'Ever visited the place?' Shane asked.

'Once, soon after we came here. The gardens and parkland are magnificent. I pushed my father round them, then left him while I visited the house.'

'The story goes,' said Shane, 'that Jane Austen's "Pemberley" in *Pride and Prejudice* was based on Chatsworth.'

Anona nodded. 'And that the "Lambton" she talks about in that book was really Bakewell.'

After passing through the attractive village of Rowsley, it was not long before Haddon Hall, with its turrets and towers and windows, could be glimpsed among the trees. 'Another stately home,' Shane commented, pulling round into the car park nearby.

Anona gazed at the building. 'My father says that the dining parlour and kitchens have hardly changed since the year 1500.'

Shane stopped the engine. 'Come on,' he said, 'we're going for a walk. Bring your jacket, it's cooler now.' Anona scrambled out, pulled on the jacket over her pink summerweight shirt and dark-blue slacks and followed Shane. He turned to wait for her, holding out his hand in a proprietorial way and grasping hers. She smiled up at him, happiness in every line of her body. He returned her smile, pressing a finger lightly against the tilted tip of her nose.

They walked up and up, turning at one point to look back at the medieval manor that was Haddon Hall. Its terraced gardens were highlighted by velvet-smooth lawns, and the brilliantly-coloured roses growing among the shrubs and trees.

Moving away from the footpath, Shane tugged Anona behind him. He found a remote spot, peeled off his jacket and spread it on the ground. Then he sat himself on it, patting the place beside him. Anona needed no second invitation. She was near enough to feel the relaxation of his limbs as his eyes wandered over the tree-scattered hills, absorbing into himself the tranquillity of the scene.

Anona could achieve no such inner peace. There was the disturbing brush of his arm against hers, the strength of his thighs revealed by the taut fit of his casual pants. From the top of her fair head to her pink-painted toenails, she responded to the sheer force of the magnetism emanating from his body. Her thoughts could not detach and wander as his were doing. Hers were purely subjective. The emotions stirring restlessly inside her were by no means aesthetic but undisguisedly physical. She wanted Shane's attention, every single bit of it, on her and her alone. If she stretched out a hand and touched his knee——?

'Haddon Hall,' Shane observed, gazing at the turreted building standing high above the River Wye, 'Haddon Hall, enveloped in the evening mist. Famous for the romance of a runaway couple way back in history.'

Anona suppressed a sigh, telling herself to be patient and went along with his train of thought. 'Lady Dorothy Vernon,' she commented, 'who eloped with Sir John Manners.'

Shane turned to her, smiling, his legs outstretched, his hands supporting his long body. 'Would you elope with the man you loved?'

His attention was all hers now, but it brought complications she could not have envisaged. 'Against my family's wishes?' she answered his question. She went on slowly,

'When that "family" is one lonely man——' She sighed. 'How can I explain? Anyway,' with a quick smile, 'the question doesn't arise, does it?'

'No, it just doesn't arise.' There were a few moments of silence, then he sat up. His head turned and again he pressed a finger against her nose. 'Impudent, that. Inviting, too.' He held her shoulders and eased her forward, kissing the end of her nose. Then he held her away, looking at her long-lashed eyes, her wide, smiling mouth, her rounded chin.

As if he could not resist the unconscious invitation in her questioning regard, his mouth covered hers and he urged her backwards until the hard ground hit her. The pressure of his body on hers was familiar, yet alien. It had been a long time since those arms had held her, since she had felt the thrusting firmness of his hips, the weight of his thighs crushing the femininity out of her so that he could drink its sweetness until replete.

Her summer shirt strained open and he was not slow to take advantage of the fact. His hand wandered, caressing the soft shape of her, then, as if still unsatisfied, pushing aside the shirt and letting his lips follow the path of his hand. The pleasure was like a pain and she whispered, 'No, Shane, no.'

Even as she heard herself utter the words, she felt herself yielding more and more. Her eyes closed as her arms crossed around his neck, but the guilt inside grew as her response to his lovemaking intensified. My father, I'm being disloyal to him, acting like a traitor ...

All the time his mouth and hands demanded more—and more—and her happiness dazzled her eyes like the sun on a cloudless day. At last it seemed he had had his fill of her, but from the look in his eyes she knew it would not be long before his mouth returned to plunder her parted lips.

'You bewitch me,' he said, his voice husky. 'You,' he flicked a curl, 'with your laughing eyes and kissable mouth, your hair like ripening corn blown about in the wind. If

I asked you to marry me, what would your answer be?'

Her hand lifted to find the back of his head and her fingers rubbed through the dark mass of his hair. The light was fading from the day and it was impossible now to see the look in his eyes. She whispered, 'Are you proposing?'

'Testing,' he taunted, covering her mouth with kisses, 'just testing.'

'I couldn't marry you,' was her gasping spoken answer. He would never be told the answer of her mind. If you asked me, her clamorous thoughts had said, I'd say 'yes, yes, please!'

In the coming of the darkness, she saw his lips harden. 'There has to be a reason,' he said sarcastically, 'for such an encouraging reply to a man as eligible and virile as I am.'

Sadness made her close her eyes. After she had spoken, he would move away and never again would they meet and kiss and make love ...

'You know it already,' she said dully.

'Your father?'

She nodded. 'He just doesn't seem to like you—I wish I knew why. He seemed to like your father.' As she had guessed, he rolled away and lay on his back. She went on, 'And you don't seem to like him. Why, Shane?' Her voice wavered a little.

'My feelings towards your father are neutral,' he said distantly.

Now the moon was rising into a black velvet sky. 'There's the other reason why I couldn't marry you.' He was silent. 'You told me yourself. You said that where women were concerned, you had no staying power.'

'True.' One word, but it made her body shiver.

'I could never marry a man I couldn't trust not to abandon me for any other woman who appealed to him.' Again he said nothing. If she had wanted him, after his curious non-proposal, there and then to confess his undying love for her and stay faithfully by her side until death did them part, then she was doomed to disappointment.

'Anyway,' she rallied, 'I told you I didn't want any more entanglements for a long time to come, not after ending my engagement to Dougal. It's not pleasant, breaking off an engagement. But,' with a goading glance at him, 'you wouldn't know, would you, since you never ever get yourself caught by a woman?'

'I wouldn't know,' he repeated tonelessly, adding coldly, 'Don't strain your brain thinking up any more reasons.' He stood, waiting for her to release his jacket, then he picked it up and pulled it on. While she struggled with hers, he turned and walked away.

Frightened that he intended leaving her to find her own way home, she ran after him. 'Shane,' she called, running to catch him up, 'Shane! Don't walk away ...'

He paused, then together but apart they made their way back to the road. In the last of the day's light, Haddon Hall stood bold and majestic, holding close the secrets of its past and whispering to those who wished to hear about those runaway lovers of so long ago.

CHAPTER SEVEN

IT was mid-morning when two large cars drew up in the filling station courtyard. Anona, who had just finished attending to a customer, looked out. One car was a sleek lavender-coloured Jaguar. The other was sprawling and familiar.

The driver who emerged from the first was undoubtedly female. Her lavender silk dress—probably chosen to match the car—clung uninhibitedly to every curve. The driver who eased out of the second car was indisputably male: the executive suit which covered his hard, substantial body passed that message on to the interested watcher.

As the couple talked beside the front car, Anona asked hoarsely, 'Who's that beautiful creature?'

'Shane's current woman,' was Rob's bad-tempered answer. 'He pulls all the females, young or old, rich or poor.'

'Is she——' Anona's tongue ran over her lips, 'rich?'

'Her father's an international banker. Her name's Lidia Harmon-Park. Need I say more?'

And was the man outside the same as the one who, last night, had made love to her on the hillside across from Haddon Hall, the man who had told her she betwitched him, who had said, in a roundabout way, If I asked, would you marry me? *Marry him?* When he had such a woman as that in his life?

A customer entered and it was while Anona was accepting his money that Shane and his companion came in. Even when the customer had gone, Anona kept her eyes averted.

'Rob,' she heard Shane say, 'get someone to take Lidia's car round the back, will you?' There were footsteps and Shane said, 'Anona?'

Her eyes lifted. They were empty. In return, his grey eyes gazed impersonally down at her. Her glance moved to inspect the young woman who leant languidly against the shop counter. The woman's hair was a mass of deep brown, draped across her forehead and falling to her shoulders. Her lips were coloured with autumn-tinted red into a perfect shape, her perfume filled the air. There was perfection in the line of her nose which possessed at its end no impudence, only a supercilious point.

'Yes, Mr Brodie?' Anona asked tonelessly.

'After Friday you won't be needed here. Albert has his doctor's permission to return to work next week. Rob will pay you the money we owe you.' Even as her heart sank she nodded calmly, as if taking the information in her stride. He rested his hands on the cash desk, his arms stiffened to support him. 'But there's a crisis approaching at Head Office.'

At once she brightened and the surge of pleasure she felt would not be pushed out of sight. It was there in her eyes as she gazed up at him. At the counter there was an impatient drumming of long, scarlet fingernails.

'My cousin Spencer,' Shane continued, ignoring his girlfriend's morse coded tapping, 'has an assistant who is expecting a child. It's not long before the baby's due and she has to leave. Is it possible for you to come and help us out there as from next Monday?'

'Part-time?'

'No, full-time.'

She uncrossed the fingers she had crossed in hope and curled her toes instead. Somehow she must harden herself to shaking her head, knowing that it would mean the end of their acquaintance. Her lips felt stiff as she said, 'Sorry, I couldn't work full-time because of my father. It would be expecting too much of the neighbours if I asked them to come in and out all day.'

Shane straightened. 'I understand,' he commented distantly, moving away. Lidia moved, too, preceding him out of the door which he closed without another glance at the watching girl inside.

It was impossible to control the trembling of her lip as she saw Lidia get into the driving seat of Shane's car while he drove hers to the repair shop at the rear. The girl moved Shane's car out of sight, handling the vehicle as if she had driven it many times. Jealousy tightened Anona's throat, but she swallowed it like unpalatable food. Taking a hold on herself, she looked quickly at Rob, hoping he had not noticed her reactions. By the sneering lift of his upper lip, it seemed he had.

'You, too?' he asked. 'How far has he got with you? Picked you up, didn't he? He found you stranded on the motorway, he said. What price did he ask for all the things he's done for you?'

She thought, I'll hit out at one of these Brodies, even if it kills me! 'A roll in the long grass,' she retorted, her eyes glittering with anger. 'Kisses—the real thing—nothing gentlemanly about them. A proposal of marriage.'

'*What?*' Rob Brodie exploded. 'You didn't take him seriously?'

'Why shouldn't I?' she challenged, enjoying Rob's discomfiture. 'Aren't I good enough for Brodie's top director?'

'That's not what I meant. Your father—isn't he Professor Willis?'

'He is, but what's that got to do with it?'

Anona held his gaze unwaveringly, but Rob looked away, apparently embarrassed.

'Nothing, nothing at all,' he said, with the look of someone who wished he hadn't spoken. A car drew up at the pumps in the courtyard and a customer got out. 'Look, Miss Willis, I didn't want you to get hurt. You just can't trust Shane.'

'With women?'

'With women, anything.'

'Do you know, Mr Brodie,' said Anona, speaking sincerely for the first time, 'I just don't believe you.'

'Okay,' Rob shrugged again, 'so you've caught him. You're engaged. Pat yourself on the back. You're the first woman to get him to propose—marriage, I mean,' he added with a sneer. 'He's made plenty of proposals of the other sort in the past.'

The shop door opened and the customer entered. To Anona's relief, the man was in such a hurry to pay he did not notice her burning cheeks and her quick breathing.

That afternoon, trade increased. The day was fine, although windy, and the tourists were out. The shop stocked confectionery and ice cream, besides other domestic items. In her spare moments, Anona helped Rob serve the mothers and children of the drivers who were busy at the self-service petrol pumps.

Anona was relieved when the time came to go home. As she walked across the courtyard, it occurred to her that Rob might have taken her claims about being engaged to his brother as being the truth. Turning, she ran back to the shop, finding it empty of customers.

'Mr Brodie.' He looked up. 'About the engagement,' she paused, uneasy that he looked so interested, 'it's not true.' She lifted her left hand. 'See, no ring.'

He laughed unpleasantly. 'No ring doesn't equal no engagement. Just give Shane time and he'll come up with a diamond-studded hunk of gold fit for a queen.'

'No, no! Don't you understand? It simply isn't true.'

Rob looked sceptical. 'None of it, not one word?'

'Well——' she hesitated. 'It's true he did propose, but——'

A waitress came through the connecting door from the self-service café. 'Mr Brodie, you're wanted,' she said. 'A customer. Says he knew you years ago and doesn't come this way often.'

'Okay, I'll be there in a minute. Here's John now.'

'Sorry I'm late,' said the young man called John. He wore a Brodie overall and was covered in grease. He took over from Anona every afternoon. 'You can go now,' he said,

FREE!

Get the exciting love-filled romances *you* want to read...
CHOOSE ONE OF THESE OFFERS NOW

4 Free Harlequin Presents!

Take these 4 FREE Harlequin Presents novels ... they are our gift to you just to introduce you to the convenience of Harlequin Reader Service, the fastest, surest way we know for you to receive the novels you love to read. As a member, you pay nothing extra for the convenience of receiving your novels by mail, no postage, no handling, no extra charges!

Your free gift includes:
Gates of Steel
by Anne Hampson
Helen entered into a loveless marriage in a mountain village in Cyprus, never dreaming she would someday find herself in a physical and emotional turmoil.

No Quarter Asked
by Janet Dailey
Stacey chose a deserted cabin in Texas to start her life over again, but she soon discovered she was an unwelcome visitor.

Sweet Revenge
by Anne Mather
He had looks, money and a castle in Portugal, but could he hold on to this elusive, strong-willed woman he craved?

Devil in a Silver Room
by Violet Winspear
Fate had brought Margo to the remote French Chateau, and now the ruthless brother of the man she had once loved, desired her.

OR choose this FREE Harlequin Catalog!

This is the catalog that lists many Harlequin novels still available to you right now. This is one handy comprehensive list for you to keep absolutely FREE — with no obligation whatsoever. If you wish, you may order from the catalog at any time. Choose the books you want to read, when you want to read them.

Send for your 4 FREE *Harlequin Presents* novels or your FREE Harlequin Catalog today

Mail the attached postage paid reply card today!

giving Anona a broad smile. 'Unless you'd like to stay and keep me company?'

Anona laughed and went on her way.

When Anona arrived home she found her father in a bright mood. His books and work had been put aside and two used cups and saucers stood on a coffee table.

'Had a visitor?' Anona asked with surprise. 'Or have the Pattersons been in?'

'Morris Brodie,' her father said, smiling. 'He called for a chat.'

Anona hid her astonishment. 'I'll call again,' Mr Brodie senior had said, and he had kept his promise.

'We didn't stop talking,' said her father, laughing. 'He was telling me all about his childhood. He's a real character, that man.'

Anona collected the empty cups.

'He's a good man, too,' Will went on, 'a good man.' He frowned. 'But he's not a well man.'

'Nor are you,' Anona reminded him.

'Maybe not,' said Will, 'but in a different way. I told him we were a couple of old crocks.'

Anona laughed and her heart lightened at the thought that her father had at last found a friend in his own age group, even though that new-found friend had, for the past eighteen months, been his sworn enemy. Anona doubted if her father had forgiven Brodie's for what one of their trucks had done to him, but it seemed that within himself he had agreed to forget.

She washed the cups and saucers and rejoined her father, sitting beside the fire which burned faintly, if smokily, in the grate.

'I've some work for you,' said Will. 'There would have been more if Morris hadn't come, but I was glad of the rest.'

Anona took the handwritten sheets.

'He says,' Will continued, 'that his son Shane's gone to

London until next week. It seems they've got an office there. They're going to expand the firm, Morris says. What's more, his son's got his eye on Europe.'

'Do you——' Anona hesitated, then plunged on, 'do you like Shane any more than you did, Father?'

He gazed across the room but was looking inward. 'Not particularly.'

'What is it about him you don't like?'

'I can't put my finger on it. There's something, somewhere, deep down in my subconscious mind, but since I'm not the one for indulging in self-analysis, I'll let it be.' He looked at her sharply. 'It doesn't matter to you that I don't like him, does it?'

Her shoulders jerked up and down in a false shrug. 'Why should it? He's been——' the word caught in her throat, 'kind to me, mending my car and so on. But it's cost him nothing, except time.' A long pause, then, when she was sure her voice would be steady, she added, 'Today he told me that after Friday they wouldn't need my help any more, so I'll be at home all day again.'

Surprising her, her father said, 'That's a pity. At least it got you out of the house for a few hours, didn't it? I've been feeling guilty about monopolising your life. At your age——'

'I know what you're going to say,' she interrupted with an indulgent sigh. 'I should be enjoying myself with people in my own age group. If I'm content, then you needn't worry, need you?'

But am I content? she asked herself. The image came to her of the face and laughing eyes of the man she had first seen overtaking her on the motorway, the man for whom she had come to feel so deeply—and so hopelessly —and she knew that she was not content. She despaired that her father still could not like him, she despaired also of ever seeing the man again.

'By the way,' Will stopped his daughter as she prepared to leave, 'Morris has invited us to his house on Saturday, just for a chat and coffee. I accepted for both of us. I assumed you wouldn't mind?' At his daughter's stunned silence, he went on, 'If you're wondering how I can go there knowing that his son shares the house with him—I did explain that the son would be away in London, didn't I?'

A sense of relief, mixed with disappointment, had her wondering whether to shake her head or nod. She could accompany her father with safety because she would not need to brace herself to meet the son of the house.

'That's fine,' she answered with false pleasure. 'It will be a wonderful change for you to get out for an hour or so.'

Pleased, her father settled back in his chair and took up his book.

Anona found her way to the tiny office between the kitchen and the living-room. She sat at his desk. Kind? she thought bitterly. Yes, Shane had been kind, with his kisses, his flattery—with his passion and his expert lovemaking ... For a few moments she rested her head on her arms on the typewriter. Recovering her composure, she began to work.

On Friday, Rob handed over an envelope containing the money Brodie's owed her.

'Still no ring?' he said, the jeering note still apparent.

'I told you, I made it all up.'

'Did you? That bit about the proposal, too?'

'Yes and no.' She pushed the envelope into her bag. 'I haven't seen Shane. He's away in London. You should know, you're his brother.'

'We lead our own lives, my wife and I. I wouldn't know what Big Brother's up to, would I? Did you know that Elsa, my wife, is in charge of Brodie's main office? And my cousin Spencer takes care of the Traffic side of the business. I don't know his movements, either.'

'Your father told us. Brodie's really do keep it all in the family, don't they?'

'In the tradition of many small family haulage firms, yes. What's wrong with that?'

'Why are you so belligerent, Mr Brodie?' she asked curiously.

'You may be going to be my sister-in-law, Miss Willis, but you've got a damned cheek talking to me like that!'

'Sorry about the second part, Mr Brodie.' Anona went to the door. 'But as I keep telling you, you're dead wrong about the first part.'

'Yeah?' Rob's smile was malicious. 'Going to do what all the other females in his life do—live with him, instead?'

'Oh!' snapped Anona, banging the shop door on the man's laughter.

On Saturday, Anona and her father had eaten their evening meal earlier than usual. When Anona asked her father if he would like to change his jacket, he said, 'It's not royalty we're visiting.'

In his heart, Anona thought, he's still the unworldly professor of archaeology, dressed for a dig in his oldest clothes. 'All the same,' she said aloud, 'it's so long since you went visiting, I thought you might wear that Harris tweed jacket you've hardly worn since you bought it.'

He looked outside, saw the sky darkening with rain clouds and said, 'You win, dear. It cost quite a lot of money, so it might as well get some wear. Especially as it looks as though it's going to be a typically British summer evening!'

Having helped her father into the jacket and pushed his chair into his ground-floor bedroom so that he could brush his hair and tie his tie in front of the mirror, Anona ran upstairs to dress. Anything will do, she thought—then checked herself, applying the same reasoning to her own clothes as she had to her father's. It was rare for her to go out for the evening, too, so she wouldn't allow the fact that Morris Brodie's son would not be present to influence her choice. For her father's sake, she told herself, she would wear an attractive dress.

In the end she wore a short-sleeved raspberry-coloured dress, vee-necked, belted, falling smoothly from the waist into neat box pleats. Round her neck she wore a choker neck chain and over the dress she pulled a cream-coloured summer jacket. Her hair remained determinedly curled, despite her efforts to tame it.

Anona was looking in her handbag for the key to the car when the telephone rang. As she said the number, she hoped the caller would not be a friend intent on a long chat. She need not have worried. The caller was terse and to the point.

'I'll be calling for you in ten minutes.'

'Shane? But your—your father said you were away.'

'I came back. Has that annoyed you? Ten minutes—is that enough time?'

'There's no need for you to come. We've got a folding wheelchair we keep in the car. And my father can just about manage the walk with crutches as far as the roadside.'

The caller, it seemed, had not listened. 'Ten minutes,' he repeated. His receiver crashed down.

Her father was not over-pleased with the news. 'Did you tell him we don't need his help?' Anona assured him she had. Will tutted. 'Arrogant, like most of his type. Young brash executive, head of the family firm. Accustomed to giving orders and expecting them to be carried out without question.'

Sad about her father's continued antagonism, even in the face of a generous and thoughtful act by the man he was condemning, she said gently, using words she knew he would appreciate, 'I have read that modern management consists not so much of autocracy and a mild form of dictatorship as attending committee meeting after committee meeting and accepting the consensus of opinion of everybody involved.'

Her father grunted, his forefinger irritably smoothing down his beard. Thus he considered the ways of the modern world and appeared to find them alien. It did not, however, seem to alter his opinion of the top director of Brodie's Transport Company.

Summoned by the rap of knuckles on the front door,

Anona opened it to see Shane waiting on the doorstep. Stiffly she said, 'It's very kind——'

'Where's your father?'

'In his usual place in the living-room. Give me time to help him out of his chair and to support himself on his crutches ...' She was talking to Shane's back. It was broad and forbidding under the loose-fitting jacket.

'Good evening, Professor Willis,' he said formally.

Her father's tone was equally reserved as he responded conversationally to the greeting. Anxious to prevent the icing over of the atmosphere even before the evening had begun, Anona said quickly, 'I'll get the car started.'

'You're coming in mine, both of you.'

'Oh. Oh well, then, I'll just go and get the wheelchair from the——'

'No need. We have a wheelchair for your father's use. We've borrowed it for the evening.'

'That's very kind,' said Anona, trying to gauge how her father was taking this exchange of views and information. She bent to lower the footrest on his chair. 'Isn't it, Father?'

'Very,' said Will, easing himself forward with the aid of a walking stick. He looked up. 'I suppose this was your idea, too, young man?'

'My father's.'

'Thoughtful man, your father. A good man. None better.' With concentrated effort, he was all the time urging himself forward.

When Shane bent down and scooped the slight, bent figure into his arms, Anona gasped and Will snapped, 'For God's sake, put me down! I will not be manhandled by anyone, let alone——'

'Father,' Anona broke in, stemming the flow of vilification which she knew would be her father's reaction, 'it's only a short distance to Shane's car. He's parked it at the curb, just behind ours.'

They were out of the cottage now and Shane was striding down the path to the gate. Anona ran to open it. When her father had been lowered with gentleness on to the back seat, she took her place beside him.

'Comfortable, Professor Willis?' Shane asked briskly, checking in the driving mirror before pulling out.

'Yes, thank you.' Will's answer was a little strangled, as though it had cost him an effort to be pleasant.

Morris Brodie was on the doorstep, rubbing his hands eagerly. He watched his son carry his unwilling burden the short distance from the drive to the front door. As they entered, followed by Anona, Morris swung the borrowed wheelchair so that it faced them.

'Put my friend Will in here, son,' he said. 'Well, well,' he took Will's hand and shook it heartily, 'you've no idea how I've been looking forward to this.'

'Me, too, Morris,' said the Professor, his face flushed by events piling one on the other. If he was ruffled by the way the easy strength of Morris Brodie's son revealed his own fragility, he managed to hide it.

'Now,' said Morris, grasping the handles of the wheel-chair, only to be waved away by his son who took over the job, 'how do you like the family home, Will?'

'If the interior can be judged by the exterior,' Will answered, 'then I shall like it extremely well. What period in time was it built, Morris?' They were in the living-room now. 'It was difficult to judge from the outside.'

Shane answered for his father. 'Roughly two centuries back, with additions and alterations.'

Will nodded without looking at the speaker. 'This room——' Will looked the length of it. 'It's fine—tasteful in every sense. My late wife would have approved.' He looked at his daughter. 'Wouldn't she, Anona?'

Anona could only nod. With Shane Brodie beside her, she felt unaccountably tongue-tied. He had scarcely looked at her since the moment they had faced each other across the doorstep.

'Now,' Morris fussed, 'what'll you have, Will? Miss Willis—or Anona, if I may be so bold?' His guests told him their preferences and Anona added, 'Please call me by my first name, Mr Brodie.'

'I'll do the honours, Father,' said Shane. 'Anona, find a seat.'

Anona remained standing. She would take no orders while a guest in the Brodie family home. The two older men settled themselves comfortably. When Shane carried over the drinks, he said softly to Anona, 'I said sit down. You have every right.'

Her lips parted in a silent gasp. 'What are you talking about?'

'Now, now, son,' Morris Brodie chided good-naturedly, 'if you must whisper sweet words in Anona's ear——'

'He's only telling me to sit down, Mr Brodie,' Anona answered, thinking quickly. 'In fact, he's *ordering* me——'

Morris laughed out loud, saying, 'He's a terror for telling people what to do, even as a young lad. We knew, his mother and I, that one day he'd take over from me. He's got all your determination, she used to say, plus a lot you haven't got. Good looks, for instance, I'd tell her back, but she would have it that *I* was handsome! Do *you* think my son's good-looking, Anona?'

The direct question came as a shock and for the first time that evening Anona was forced to look directly at the son of the house. What could she say? I think he's the most attractive, devastatingly good-looking man I've ever met? That I wish he really had proposed to me the other day? That I love him and—*Love him*?

The mocking eyes into which she looked had surely not read her mind? The curve of his mouth was less of a smile than an expression of cynicism. Cynical towards her? For what reason? Had he not forgiven her for implying she couldn't trust him not to forsake her if he really had been suggesting marriage?

Shane drawled, 'She's taking so long making up her mind, she's probably wondering how to break it to you that she thinks I'm as ugly as sin.'

'No, no, I don't. I think you're very attractive——' Turning a deep pink, she realised what she had said. The words had tumbled over themselves in their determination to be spoken.

Will Willis's smile was impersonal and short-lived. He might have forgiven the owner of Brodie's, but he still carried on a vendetta against the son who was the man in charge of the company.

Morris, however, laughed heartily at Anona's comments. Shane, whose eyes were hooded as they gazed at Anona's warm cheeks, said, 'The compliment's returned.'

Will asked, as if resenting the praise of his daughter by the man on whom his hatred of Brodie's was now concentrated, 'What about your other son, Morris?'

'Ah, yes—Rob,' Morris answered, 'younger than Shane. A good lad, but less up here.' He tapped his head. 'Jealous of his elder brother. He always was. He'd like to have Shane's brains and he'd like Shane's way with the girls.'

Frowning, Anona said, 'But isn't your other son married, Mr Brodie? He mentioned that Elsa—I think that was her name——' Morris nodded, 'is in charge of the main office.'

'Elsa, yes.' Morris rubbed his chin. 'Nice girl, but nothing special. She makes up in intelligence and common sense what she lacks in looks.'

Shane lounged back in his chair, legs outstretched, hands in pockets, broad shoulders pushed back against the chair. He said, smiling faintly, 'You see, Anona, how much importance my father attaches to brain-power.'

'I most certainly do,' Morris Brodie exclaimed. 'Which is why I had you educated, my lad.' To Will, 'He climbed right up the educational ladder, came out of it with honours —then I put him down at rock bottom in the family firm.'

'Literally', said Shane, smiling. 'He held out a book of instructions, put a spanner in my hand and pushed me down under all the trucks and cars he could find.'

'Did he resent it!' said Morris, smiling. 'But he came through that, too,' he added with pride.

Anona looked for approval from her father at Shane's accomplishments. She found instead a compressed hardness of the lips, eyes that stared at the patterned carpet which his feet could not touch.

'This daughter of yours, Will—she's no fool, is she?' Morris commented.

'I'll echo that,' said Shane, lifting his glass to his lips and watching Anona enigmatically over its rim.

'What do you mean by that?' Anona demanded, but Shane merely continued to watch her.

'They mean you're intelligent, dear,' said her father, savouring his drink. 'My one sorrow, Morris, is that she hasn't inherited my love of archaeology. She's observant and painstaking enough to have made a good one. Patient, too,' he stated with a sigh. 'She has to be, to cope with me. Since my accident I've been a very trying per——' He stopped, remembering where he was, who his hosts were, what they, through one of their trucks, had done to him.

Shane put aside his glass and stood up. His shirt was of silk, his tie likewise, and a mixture of blue and grey. 'Anona.' Startled, she looked up. 'The garden's a pleasant place at this time of the year.'

It was a hint, heavy and not, it seemed, to be ignored.

'That's right, Shane, take Anona for a breath of air. Us two young men,' Morris indicated himself and Will, then laughed at his own joke, 'we'll chat about the old days.'

Anona looked at her father as if seeking his permission, but in reality to discover his feelings. He gave a faint nod. In the circumstances, there was little else he could do.

The garden was large and wide, the lawn being edged with beds of glowing-coloured flowers. Trees stood in a long line behind them, marking the boundary of the land. Near the end of the garden, its branches outspread over the lawn, stood a giant mulberry tree. It was here that Shane stopped, facing Anona. While she had commented on the scents of the flowers, Shane had remained preoccupied.

Now he spoke and his words shocked her into forgetting

their surroundings. He said, his voice grating against the background of birdsong and peace, 'I've been informed that we're engaged to be married.'

Anona's heart began to thud. 'Who told you that?'

'The man *you* told—my brother.'

She started to protest, then shrugged. 'I did tell Rob you'd proposed—which you did in a roundabout sort of way. You can't deny it.' Shane said nothing. 'I only told him about it because——' she stopped, not knowing how to explain.

'Please go on.'

'Oh——' Her sigh was short and angry. She was committed now. 'I just felt I had to hit out—at a Brodie, that's all. Rob was being nasty, making—making innuendoes. You'd just told me I wasn't wanted any more.'

'And that upset you?'

If she had told him just how much it had upset her, not to mention how jealous she had been of his attractive female companion, he would laugh at her and pity her and congratulate himself on yet another conquest. She was silent. 'What innuendoes did Rob make?' he probed.

She could not keep ignoring his question. 'He implied you'd picked me up, as you did, of course, but he meant in the sense that——'

'I know what you mean. That you were standing by the roadside offering your—er—services.'

'Which is what you thought yourself at first, wasn't it?' He nodded. His hand came out and he lifted her chin. In the gathering darkness he moved, putting his lips against hers, brushing them backwards, forwards, until she found herself straining to catch his mouth and hold it. It was instinct, she insisted silently, a reflex action. When his arms went round her, the hardness in them crushing her to him, it was impossible to disguise her pleasure at being back where her body seemed to have decided it belonged.

His lips forced hers apart and with a growing delight she allowed the kiss to search and delve, clasping him around his neck as though clinging to his very substance for life-support. As the kiss ended and he lifted his head, she wished she could see his eyes and judge whether her response had pleased him or earned his contempt. Seconds later, she knew the answer.

'We're engaged,' he said roughly. 'You understand?'

'No,' she said quietly, choking back her disappointment at his attitude after such a kiss, 'I don't understand.'

'Rob rang me at the London office to congratulate me,' he explained, an edge to his voice. 'He thought I'd swear at him for getting me so deeply involved with a woman. Instead I thanked him kindly for letting me know how the girl I wanted to marry felt about me.'

His arms around her tightened, but she pulled back. 'You *don't* know how I feel about you. I told Rob it wasn't true.'

He looked into her face which was a mouth's touch from his. 'What wasn't true?'

'That you'd proposed to me. I know you did mention marriage, but only as a kind of joke. Testing, you called it, although you didn't explain just what you were testing.'

'Your reaction.' His breath was warm on her lips. 'Tell me something, my bright-eyed girl. Do you love me?'

'Yes, but——' Her breath was a gasp. She had confessed to a love for him which she had not even been conscious of feeling. Yet it was true. Now that she had allowed herself to admit the fact, she knew it had been true for a long time —almost from the moment they had met, before that maybe, when those laughing eyes had mocked her as they passed her on that motorway ...

Those eyes were bright now, lit with a taunting triumph through having so cleverly forced the confession from her. 'No buts, my love. You're mine. You're marrying me.'

Her efforts to escape made his hold on her tighten. 'You're going too fast,' she protested. 'There's Lidia, the woman you brought to the garage. *She's* your woman— Rob told me. Her father's a banker, up to his eyebrows in money.' Still she struggled, and still he held her, his arms bands of steel. 'And money's what you're after, isn't it? Brodie's may be flourishing now, but we all know what happens so often to family firms, don't we? They fail, they become bankrupt ...'

His teeth gritted. 'I'll close that spiteful mouth of yours if it takes me till midnight!' The kiss he gave her this time was meant not to be enjoyed but endured. It was punishing and savage, leaving her lips bruised and throbbing.

'That wasn't fair,' she remonstrated. 'What I said was the truth. Rob implied——'

'Rob *implies* a lot of things. It's his way of getting at me. There's very little brotherly love between us.'

'All right,' she forced a sigh, 'there's the other thing. You told me yourself, so you can't deny it—that you couldn't stay faithful to a woman for long. That first day we met and you told me you were "mine" if I said the word. You meant it as a joke, of course, but I said that when—if—I ever married, I'd want a man who'd be faithful.'

'I'll be faithful, sweetheart,' his hand eased down to her waist and rested on her hip, 'by heaven, I'll be faithful. When a man's found the one he's been looking for, he never leaves her, never lets her go. Now will you marry me?'

There was a song in her head that deafened her with its sweetness. 'Nothing—nothing will stop me,' she whispered, resting her hands against the wall of his chest.

'Not even your father?'

She sobered, her eyes following the ridge of his jaw and wondering, in the semi-darkness, if bristles had already started to grow. 'I don't know.' Her voice was small and uncertain.

His hands cupped her face and his lips rested against hers. A moment later he said, 'Let's go and see, shall we?'

Hand in hand, they entered the living-room. Morris looked up, eyes hopeful, waiting. He knew about them, Shane had said. Will Willis looked up too. There was no eagerness in his eyes. Instead they held surprise which changed to disbelief which in turn gave way to a kind of horror.

'Anona?' Her name was spoken sharply, as a reprimand which carried her straight back to childhood when she had displeased the distinguished, rather remote man who was her father.

Her fingers tightened involuntarily around Shane's. He felt the pressure and knew at once of her fear. Gently he pulled her across the room to stand in front of her father. She thought wildly, Shane's his enemy. After he knows about Shane and myself, will I become my father's enemy, too? The thought frightened her and her reaction was to try to disengage her hand from Shane's. His grip tightened.

'Professor Willis,' said Shane, 'do I have your permission to marry your daughter?'

Morris heaved his solid length from his chair and brought his hand down in a warm paternal thud on his son's back. 'You're a good lad, Shane. There's not many young men who ask their prospective father-in-law's permission these days, is there, Will?'

Will's eyes went from Morris to his son and finally to his daughter. He was caught in a trap and as three pairs of eyes fixed on him, there was no doubt that he was aware of it. *Brodie's*, Anona could hear her father's voice after he had been told by doctors that he would never walk normally again, *I'd like to tear them apart, all of them, bring them to their knees and ruin them just like they've ruined me* ...

Now he was being asked to approve of the marriage of his daughter to the owner's son, to the man who was also now the head of the company. His eyes sought those of his daughter, and she was chilled by the look in them. 'You wish to marry this man?'

Her lips were dry. She tried to moisten them with a parched tongue. 'Father, I——' Shane must have sensed her inability to deal with the situation and his fingers tightened again round hers.

'Yes, Father,' she whispered at last, 'I do.'

CHAPTER EIGHT

THERE was a pause. The man at whom all three stared started to smile. There was a curve to his lips, a shaking hand was outstretched to hold his daughter's—but his eyes were like those of a man who had been dealt a death-blow.

Morris saw only the smile and the shaking hand—shaking with joy as he probably thought, Anona reflected, as she put her hand into her father's and bent to kiss his cheek. She whispered, 'I do love him, Father. It just—happened that way.'

Shane stepped in, taking Will Willis's hand. 'Thank you,' he said simply.

Will nodded and the smile grew stronger, his grip strengthening too as he shook the younger hand that rested in his. 'I hope you'll come to treasure her as I do.'

Morris, as well as Shane, knew that Will had fought a battle and conquered, freeing himself at last from his deeply embedded resentment aginst the Brodie family. There was laughter and congratulations and through it all Anona hid her bewilderment at the turn of events. Champagne was drunk, with toasts to the engaged couple's future and to the newly-formed friendship between the two older men. Yet Anona remained dazed, wondering when she would awaken from her dream.

It was later, as they drank coffee, that Morris said, 'Have you mentioned to Anona about Spencer's assistant having to be off work?'

Shane and Anona exchanged glances and Shane's eyebrow lifted. 'Have I, Anona?' Anona nodded, then Shane pretended to rub his cheek in puzzlement. 'Let me see, what was your answer?'

111

'You know what it was,' Anona retorted, remembering with a shock the changed situation.

'Well, stop fooling, lad,' said Morris. 'Was it yes or no?'

Embarrassed, Anona answered for Shane. 'I said no, Mr Brodie, but——' She glanced at her father. 'You see, I didn't want to be away from home for too many hours.'

'You were thinking of your dad?' To Will, 'She's a good daughter. I hope she's going to be a good daughter to me, too.' He slapped his knee with his big hand and laughed. 'It won't be long before you've got two fathers to fuss over.'

Will laughed, seeming to like the idea. This puzzled Anona. If he had forgiven the owner of Brodie's so completely, why didn't that forgiveness extend to the owner's son?

'Help them out at the office, Anona,' said Will, handing her his cup and saucer which she put beside her own. 'I've no objection. The Pattersons would be willing to look after me, feed me, and so on. They don't do it for nothing, and they're pleased with the small amount of money I'm able to give them.'

'So what's the answer now?' asked Shane, eyes mocking. 'Shall we keep it all in the family as tradition dictates?'

'All in the family,' Anona agreed, adding quickly, 'now I know my father has no objection.'

'Good.' Morris sat again and rested his hands on his knees. 'It's in the Traffic Department—I expect Shane told you. It might seem a bit complicated at first, but Spencer's good at explaining. Usual pay, eh, Shane?' he asked with a twinkle.

Shane was reclining in his armchair, arms folded, eyelids drooping as his gaze ran over the girl they were discussing. 'A bit more, I think, don't you? After all, she's a superior being, this new assistant of ours. She's going to be the boss's wife.'

Anona looked with some anxiety at her father, but he was smiling, too.

'I've been thinking,' said Morris, turning to Will. 'You're

writing a book, aren't you?' Will nodded. 'Now Shane and Anona are engaged, they'll want a bit of time together in the evenings. I know a woman in the village,' Morris continued, 'who's a very good typist. She used to work for the local solicitor, so she's got it up there.' In a now familiar gesture he tapped his head. 'She left to look after her aged mother. Sad to say, her mother died—she was over ninety —and the lady's at a loose end. Fed up with having nothing to do, she told me when I met her in the post office. She's a widow and fiftyish—your age, Will?'

'More or less,' Will answered.

'She'd come in a few hours a day and do anything you wanted. She's used to invalids, you see.'

Anona flinched for her father's sake, but he appeared not to mind his friend's bluntness. It seemed he was accepting the situation at last.

'What would her name be?' Will enquired. He spoke as if the idea appealed to him.

'May Howton. Lives in a cottage about half a mile from the village. Goes around on a bicycle.'

'I think I've seen her when I've been shopping,' Anona said. 'She waves each time I overtake her in my car.'

'That's the lady,' said Morris, happily. 'Will, I'm sure you'll like her. I could drive round and see her and ask her to call on you. Would you like that idea?'

Will laughed. 'You wouldn't be pressuring me, Morris?'

'Not much,' said Shane, smiling blandly. 'Forceful character, my father. Come on, my love,' his hand extended towards Anona, 'come and see my suite of rooms and leave these two to arrange each other's lives.'

'That's right,' said the irrepressible Morris, 'take the girl to see your etchings.' He affected a frown. 'What's an etching, Will?'

'It's a kind of drawing on a metal plate coated with wax and resin and immersed ...'

As the door closed, their voices faded. Shane smiled at

Anona and she responded, feeling her heart bound with a happiness she had never known before. He took her hand and pulled her to the foot of the staircase, then behind him to the top.

It was the living-room they entered first. It had been modernised, but the room still retained an atmosphere of the past, with its ceiling beam and delicate mouldings. The fireplace had been converted into a wide tiled alcove and into it had been fitted a television set and corner fitments.

The carpet was patterned in autumnal colours. Arm-chairs were velvet-covered in dull gold. A low circular inlaid table was plainly an antique of some value. The whole gave a sense of expensive yet tasteful comfort which beckoned a visitor inside. 'Do you approve?' Shane asked, and Anona nodded.

He returned to the landing, inviting her to follow, and opened the door of the adjoining room. 'This is where I sleep,' he said. 'And where one day before very long, you'll join me.'

To hide her confusion at his words, she strolled to the window, then turned to lean against it, surveying the room at a distance. The double bed was covered by a richly embossed quilt. There was a wall of fitted wardrobes, a tasteful dressing-table and matching chest of drawers, a floor-to-ceiling bookcase filled with books. Through a door she glimpsed a bathroom tiled in pale green.

She thought of her own cramped bedroom at the cottage and sighed. He strolled towards her. 'Why the sadness, sweet?' His arms went loosely round her waist. 'Soon all this will be yours, too.'

Slowly she turned in his arms away from him and gazed out of the window. 'I'm not sure, Shane.' There was a waver in her voice. 'I'm worried about what's going to happen to my father in the future. I can't leave him alone to cope——'

Shane's hands on her waist spun her round, his fingers outspread on her slim hips. 'My father had an idea which by now he has probably discussed with your father—that he could come here to live, sharing the house. It would be company for my father and vice versa, not to mention being more comfortable than the cottage you're living in.'

She ran a finger along the diagonal lines of his tie. 'I still don't know, Shane.'

'Do you object to your father living here, then?'

'No, not at all. How could I?' She sought his eyes, trying to explain. 'It's just that—everything's happening too fast. I remember all the things my father's said about Brodie's, how he'd hold a life-long grudge against the company for what it did to him. Yet here we are, you and I, engaged to be married. And there you are, calmly suggesting that the man from whom Brodie's took away so much might come here and live. Live with the Brodie family! You don't know what you're asking, Shane.'

'I know what I'm asking. I'm asking a beautiful girl called Anona Willis to share my life and my bed. To *marry* me——'

The thought struck her and eyes widened in fear. 'To take your name!'

Shane thrust her away in anger.

'You don't understand, Shane,' she defended herself. 'For eighteen months and more I've heard the name of Brodie cursed and abused by my father. Now I'm being asked to adjust to hearing it used as my own name.'

Shane said bitterly, 'Earlier you admitted you loved me. Is this what you call love?'

She looked at him, seeing his thick dark hair, his black eyebrows almost meeting in his anger, the faintly flaring nostrils, the full, demanding lips. There was his ridged jaw and—yes, bristles were already forming a shadow around his chin. Her hand lifted as it had longed to do earlier and her fingers rubbed against the roughness.

'Shane,' she said huskily, 'oh, Shane——' Her hand dropped away. 'Make me believe my fears are groundless. Do something, anything . . .'

His eyes fired to life. 'I need,' he said, 'no greater encouragement than that.' His hands found her armpits and he lifted her backwards towards the bed. Its edge was behind her knees and she felt herself falling backwards on to it. Her legs were being raised until she was lying full-length, then the man she loved was stretched beside her.

His arms slid beneath her, pulling her round and on to her side. His fingers ran along her spine, forcing her to arch her body towards him. Her hands gripped his shoulders and her fingertips pressed into the muscle there, sinewy and strong from turning giant steering wheels and manoeuvring monster-sized trucks.

Beneath the silk of his shirt she could feel the dark chest hairs springing, the ridges of his collarbone and, above his shirt collar, the suntanned throat. As his caresses grew more intimate, the stiffness that had made her tense eased away. Their bodies touched, thigh against thigh, hips pressed to hips, her breasts crushed against the unyielding wall of his chest.

He held her from him and looked into her flushed face. 'I want you, woman,' he said huskily. 'Give, for God's sake, give. Where's the warm and ardent girl I kissed out there in the garden?' The hands on her shoulders shook her, then his mouth covered hers and the desire in her flared at last into a dancing flame. Her pulses throbbed as his mouth invaded hers with an intimacy and unequivocal possession that made her tremble. His hand moved to find her neckline, slipping beneath the fabric and finding the silky softness of her breasts.

'Shane, oh, Shane, I love you . . .' The confession burst from her like water flooding over a dam. She was caught in its onward flow, helpless but ecstatic as she abandoned herself to the high-reaching tide of his lovemaking. Her arms clung in total submission as she cried, 'If you want to love me, I don't care, I don't care, because I love you and want you so much . . .'

He murmured endearments, his lips burning a trail from throat to neck-hollows and down, down to the shadowed cleft which still felt the imprint of his demanding mouth. He eased away, a light in his smiling eyes, his hand stroking the fair, disordered hair, his mouth touching her bright eyes, the tip of her nose. His finger stroked across her lips.

'Why the downward curve, my love? Are you disappointed about my refusal to accept your invitation?'

The tension regained its hold as she sensed cynicism beneath the words. Colour swept over her cheeks, deepening the flush his love-caresses had created. Now it was the colour and anger of self-defence. 'What invitation?' she bluffed. 'If I said anything to encourage you, it was in the heat of the moment. I didn't mean a word.' She eased away as if she could not bear to be in contact with him.

Shane reached out and jerked her back against him. 'You meant everything you said. You're mine, do you hear? Soon this,' he lifted her left hand, 'will wear my ring. When it's joined by a plain gold band, you'll be my wife, my woman.'

'One of your many women.' As his eyebrow lifted she added, 'Second to Lidia, who has the money as well as the social status you need for the family business.'

'Why, you——' He gripped her wrist and forced it backwards and upwards behind her.

She cried out in agony. 'Let me go! I hate you!'

His mouth descended again, bullying, savaging, teeth against teeth until she moved her jaw and allowed him access. As his ardour increased, he released her arm and in an ecstasy of loving the freed arm gripped his waist, feeling the leanness beneath the leather belt, and moving over the muscle-taut torso she had first glimpsed on the motorway.

At last he released her, swinging off the bed and straightening his tie. He stood, hands on hips, breathing regular and deep. He smiled tauntingly. 'Now do you hate me?'

'How could I, when I love you?' She gazed up at him, missing already the warmth and strength of him beside her.

He smiled and it was as though he had won a contest. He walked to a mirror, picking up a hairbrush and running it over his hair.

Anona lay watching him. She felt exhausted with a satisfied exhaustion, used, drained, yet aware of a lurking tension which, inexperienced as she was in close relationships with the male of the species, she couldn't understand.

He approached and his hand came out. 'Come, my sweet. You're tempting me far more than you know by lying there as if you're waiting to be seduced.'

He laughed at her annoyance as she gave him a look of scorn mingled with injured pride. 'I've never begged for any man—and never will,' she declared, finding the floor with her feet and standing unsteadily.

'No?' Shane returned softly. 'One day you'll discover otherwise. I'll make love to you, then I'll leave you alone. *Then* you'll come begging to me, pleading with me to——'

Her hands lifted to cover her ears and he laughed. She looked towards the mirror and exclaimed at her untidiness. 'Is there a comb I could borrow, Shane?' she asked with a touch of shyness.

He opened a drawer and took out a large pink one. 'Pink for a girl. I keep it especially for all the women I invite to my bedroom,' he mocked.

Anona accepted it, inspecting it closely.

Shane asked with amusement, 'Looking for long brown hairs, each one bearing the name Lidia? You won't find any.' He taunted again, 'The comb is washed regularly by the housekeeper who comes in daily from the village. That way it's always ready for the next—sleeping partner.'

Her head lifted sharply. 'So you really mean it. You do have women up here?'

'Talk in the past tense, my love,' he drawled. 'I told you, I'm no untried youth.'

'Which means that Lidia is one of your women?'

He was becoming annoyed. 'If jealousy means that you really do love me, then long may your jealousy continue.

All the same, whatever happened in my private life before we met isn't your concern.'

'Before we met? But only the other day Lidia was with you at the filling station.'

He twisted the comb from her fingers and sank its teeth into her hair, pulling at the tangled curls until she shrieked with pain. 'Stop, please stop!' Her hands lifted to protect herself.

'If you say you're sorry.'

'I'm sorry, but I don't know why.'

He gave her back the comb and watched, hands in pockets, as she rubbed her head, then combed her hair. 'My powder's in my bag and that's downstairs.'

'I can't provide that,' he said, and she flashed him a smile.

'I didn't expect you could,' she answered. 'You're all man.' This time her smile was deliberately provocative and he dived for her, but she eluded him and wrenched open the door, speeding down the stairs.

'You'll pay for that,' he breathed, catching her up and putting his arm round her waist. 'One day, when you're at my mercy.'

She put a finger to her lips and they entered the living-room.

'That's settled, then,' Morris was saying. 'When you two marry, Will's agreed to move in here.'

Anona's arms went round her father's neck. 'Are you sure? You won't miss the cottage?'

'I might,' Will answered with a shrug. 'But sooner that than live there alone. Not that I mind my own company—if only I could w——' There it was again, the forbidden subject.

'We'll make sure you won't miss the cottage,' Morris broke in. 'Here you'll have peace and quiet—and the good lady from the village to type your work.' To his son, he said, 'We called May Howton on the phone and she said

she'd be very pleased to work for Will. Anona, May promised to call on your father on Monday, the day you start
work in our Traffic Department. Have I done right,
Shane?'

His son nodded. 'I'm returning to our London office on
Monday.'

'So soon?' Anona asked, her disappointment showing.

'Sorry, my sweet.' His arm went round her. 'I wasn't due
back here until midweek—I'm in the middle of some delicate negotiations. I came home to propose to you. And that,'
he added with a glint, 'was the most delicate negotiation of
all.'

There was general laughter, started by Morris who threw
back his head, enjoying the joke, enjoying life in his usual
hearty way.

Will yawned and Morris noticed. 'Take them back,
Shane. Go somewhere and say a fond goodnight to your
beloved, then come back for your future father-in-law.'

Did her father flinch? Anona caught a movement, but
there was no chance to check as Shane had her hand and
was leading her from the room.

He kissed her lingeringly. 'Tomorrow afternoon? We'll
go for a drive into the country.'

She rested her head against his chest, hearing the drumming of his heart. 'Why is tomorrow such a long way off?'
she said, her lips soft-touching his shirt. It did not matter
now how much she hinted at the depth of her love for him,
nor the fact that he was as necessary to her happiness as
the sun's heat to a plant's growth.

He lifted her chin and his grey eyes probed the ocean
depths of hers. 'We could make it tonight, my love. Get
your father to bed, slip out and I'll be waiting in my car to
carry you to my lair. We could make love, become as man
and wife . . .'

'Hush!' Her hand covered his mouth. 'I couldn't leave
the cottage without telling my father. I wouldn't have a
moment's peace.'

'Just an hour or two?' He pressed her palm to his lips, then pulled her against him again, so that every curve of her body fitted into every angle of his.

Shaking her head she answered, 'Until tomorrow. I'll be patient, as long as you promise to be patient, too.'

'Impatiently patient,' he said, smiling, and releasing her.

When Shane called for Anona the next afternoon, Will greeted him with only a trace of reserve. The day was warm and before they left, Shane wheeled Will into the back garden. If necessary, Will said, he could shout to the neighbours and they would help him back into the cottage. They had, in any case, promised to bring him a cup of tea during the afternoon.

'Where are we going?' Anona asked, eyes bright, mouth curved with happiness.

'In the same direction as before, except that this time we'll make for the Blue John Caverns.'

'But Shane,' she looked down at her feet, 'my sandals won't stand up to going round the caverns. If I'd known . . .'

'I don't intend going into them. We'll leave that for another day.' He gave her a quick grin. 'I'm a newly-engaged man. I want my wife-to-be to myself. A little privacy, a lot of love . . .'

'Mm,' Anona pretended to consider the matter, 'a kiss or two maybe to keep you going till you get back from London.'

'Thursday's a long way away, my love. One or two won't be enough. And no arguments.'

He parked amongst the other cars in the special parking area within sight of Mam Tor. 'We'll patronise the shop down there,' Shane commented.

'Pretending we're tourists?' Anona asked, catching Shane's hand and delighting in her new freedom to do so.

'Why not? It's years since I came here, anyway.'

The shop contained dishes, ornaments and gold and silver jewellery. The stone common to most of them was Blue

John, multicoloured and rare. The area, the leaflet explained, was thought to be the world's only known source of the stone. The caves in which the stone was found were mined many centuries before by the Romans.

'Choose a ring,' Shane told Anona, as they entered the shop. 'It will take the place of an engagement ring until we're able to go together to buy one.'

'Set in silver?' Anona asked, uncertain as to the price Shane was willing to pay.

'Gold. This is attractive.' He spoke to an assistant who proved anxious to please. Shane pushed the ring he had chosen on to Anona's engagement finger. 'A bit too loose.'

The assistant found another in a smaller size. The stone's gold setting was simple in design. Shane took Anona's hand again and the ring was a perfect fit. 'A pendant?' Shane asked. 'Set in gold, too.'

'But Shane, you're spending too much!'

'I'm the best judge of that,' he dismissed, and Anona felt put down.

'Flaunting your wealth for the world to see?' she goaded, retaliating.

'I'll deal with you later,' he returned blandly, and the assistant smiled.

A pendant was chosen to match the ring. When the money was handed over, they left the shop. The ring was on Anona's finger, the pendant in a box in Shane's pocket. As they climbed the steep slope to the road Anona asked, 'Where now?'

'We're going for a walk.' He gazed across to Mam Tor and they made for the grassland across the busy road, finding a deep hollow which was well out of sight of straying tourists. Shane removed his jacket, spreading it on the springy turf. Anona dropped down to sit, knees drawn up, her arms wrapped around her legs. She was glad she had decided to wear jeans and short-sleeved shirt. Their casualness matched Shane's jeans and his open-necked sports shirt.

From his pocket Shane pulled out the box containing the pendant. He sat beside her saying, 'Turn around, my blue-eyed girl.' He lifted the abundance of fair hair and fastened the pendant, letting his fingers trail her neck, lightly skimming it until a shiver ran through her.

His hands found her throat, slipping down, down to search for the womanly curves of her body. With a catch of her breath she leaned back against him, resting against his chest.

'Shane,' she whispered, 'Shane ...' Hands which were strong enough to control a truck moved gently over the softly rounded shape of her. When he found the twin points of her breasts she gave a little cry of ecstasy and reached up and back to clasp her hands behind his neck, abandoning herself to the infinite pleasure of his caresses.

Then she found herself twisted round and lying full-length on her back. He was beside her, then above her, and his kisses were rough, his lips mobile and strong. Their legs entwined, their mouths clung. His hands stroked and cajoled and coaxed from her a passionate, uninhibted response.

Her hands had slipped under his shirt to stroke his waist and hard, hair-covered chest. He was murmuring her name over and over again and she moaned in her ecstasy. 'My love, my love,' his mouth moved against her ear, 'I want you so much.'

The words quickened her breathing, put fire in her eyes. Then reason intruded, bursting her bubble of delight. She became aware of the hard ground beneath, of the open air, of the sound of distant laughter. 'Not now, darling. We can't, we mustn't ...'

'You're mine, my love, my wife. Why not?'

Did he know what he was saying? 'When—when you're my husband, Shane.'

'Couples don't wait.' His hungry lips were burning a path across her throat, then fastened brief and hard on her lips. 'Not couples who are in love with each other as we are,' he insisted, and his kiss deepened, pinning her to the grass-covered ground and bringing her arms to cross around his neck.

His head was raised at last. When he gazed into her long-lashed eyes, pushing back her hair and tracing her wide mouth with his finger, he must have sensed her vulnerability.

'I'll take pity on you this once. It's neither the time nor the place for the ultimate realisation of our love. But,' his lips tingled life into her ear, 'I'm not a patient man. What I want I have, and I want you.' His emphasis on the last three words flooded her eyes with gladness, superseded by a shy pleading and muted repudiation of his words.

He laughed. 'Now she wants me, now she doesn't. I get the message in your changing expressions.' He lifted himself from her and stood, holding out his hand for her to grip. He hauled her upright and turned her round, brushing her shirt and jeans free of pieces.

'Tomorrow morning,' Shane explained as they drove home, 'you'll be meeting Spencer. He takes care of the Traffic Department.'

'Is he a Brodie, too?'

'He is.' He gave her a quick smile. 'Say your bit about keeping it all in the family.'

Anona smiled and shook her head.

Shane went on, 'He's my father's brother's son. My cousin, in fact. He's a couple of years younger than I am. He holds a heavy goods vehicle driving licence, too. I think he prefers truck driving to a desk job, so he often puts himself on the driving schedule.'

Anona frowned. 'Which means that some of his responsibilities must fall on his assistants?'

'It does. But,' his hand strayed to her thigh—a possessive action on his part which made her heartbeats trip—'I have complete confidence in the girl who's going to help him out temporarily as his assistant.'

In response, Anona covered his hand with hers.

Shane refused Anona's offer of coffee or a drink. Instead, he kissed her with a thoroughness and touched her with an intimacy which were, in themselves, a demonstration of ownership.

'Are you telling me,' she said, her voice husky with emotion, 'that I'm yours and no other's?'

He pinched her chin and tantalised her lips with the tip of his tongue. 'I certainly am, sweetheart. Remember that, will you?'

'I wouldn't even want to forget. I want to belong to you, haven't you guessed that by now?' She seized the hand that held her chin and pretended to bite his finger.

He evaded her sharp teeth easily. 'Imp,' he accused, 'temptress! You think you're safe, don't you, sitting in a car outside your father's cottage. What's to stop me driving on——'

'Shane, I must go. Suppose the neighbours are looking?'

'What's wrong with a man kissing a girl he's engaged to? Anyway, all the world loves a love scene, especially when the story has a happy ending.'

Anona straightened as Shane released her. There was a faint movement of the curtains in the living-room of the cottage. Was her father watching them? Catching Shane's hand with both of hers, she asked, 'Will ours have a happy ending?' A whisper of anxiety twitched at the veil in her mind which hid the future.

Shane's hand stiffened between hers. 'I see no reason why it shouldn't, do you?' It was as though he was already retreating from her behind that veil.

'None at all,' she answered, reaching up for a last kiss. His response was possessive enough and powerful enough to have torn down any barrier, even if it had been made of the hardest rock in the world.

Spencer Brodie was unlike his two cousins in almost every way, the exception being a certain facial similarity. His hair was red, whereas Shane and Rob were dark-haired.

Spencer was of medium height, whereas Shane and Rob were tall. Spencer welcomed Anona with gratitude, saying that he doubted if he could have managed without her.

Anona had entered the red-brick building by the main entrance, asking at the enquiries desk for the Traffic Department, and explaining her reason for being there.

'In that case,' the girl had said, 'there's no need for you to see Mrs Rob——' the girl had smiled at Anona's frown, 'Mrs Rob Brodie, that is—Mr Rob's wife. She's in charge of the main office. I expect Mr Spencer Brodie's expecting you.'

'What a lot of Brodies,' Anona commented, smiling with the girl and thanking her.

Spencer explained that not only was his assistant away, but that there was a vacancy for a traffic clerk to manage the local work.

'We have two sections,' he explained. 'Long-distance which you will do, and local deliveries. Until we get someone capable and efficient, I'm tied up in running that side.

'Normally,' he went on, 'customers telephone us with their instructions a day or so before they want the work carried out. They mail us with written confirmation of the orders. Our regular customers know about the "Conditions of Carriage", so they don't expect any acknowledgement from us.'

Anona nodded, hoping she would remember everything Spencer was telling her. 'What about new customers?' she asked.

The door opened quietly, but she was straining too hard to listen to the speaker to turn round.

'Well, new customers or, as we say, "one off" customers, are told of the "Conditions of Carriage" before the work is carried out by us.'

'So what happens,' Anona asked, 'when you receive the orders?'

'A traffic clerk—you, in the case of long-distance work—prepares a four-part set which includes the invoice, consignees' copy—that is, the firm or person receiving the goods—the receipt note and file copy.'

A familiar voice came from behind them and Anona's heart bounded. She swung round to see Shane, dressed for his executive role, yet smiling and relaxed.

'The driver,' he said, temporarily taking Spencer's place as teacher, 'is given the consignees' copy and the receipt note—on this he gets a signature for the safe delivery of the goods. Traffic clerks feed drivers with orders when they return empty during the day. So now you know, my love.' He came across and put his arm round her. 'But there's still a lot for you to learn.'

'Don't frighten her,' warned Spencer, smiling, 'I need her help too much.'

'Shane!' Anona said, her eyes shining. 'I didn't expect to see you.'

'Surprise, surprise,' he remarked dryly, and kissed her thoroughly under the astonished eyes of Spencer Brodie. 'I couldn't leave without my goodbye kiss,' he said, letting her go but keeping an arm around her waist. 'Spencer, meet my bride-to-be.'

It would surely be impossible, Anona thought, for Spencer's eyes to open any wider. He pointed. 'You don't mean you—she——'

'It's true,' said Anona. 'We're engaged.' She looked with shy, admiring eyes at the strong, handsome profile of the man beside her.

'So the rumours were wrong,' Spencer said, still bemused. 'It wasn't Lidia after all.'

'It was not Lidia,' said Shane firmly, ending the discussion. He looked at his watch. 'I must be on my way back to London.'

'What part?' Spencer asked.

'Central. Why?'

'If I'd known ... There's a load to go to West London tomorrow. The delivery could have been brought forward.

Having a bit of trouble working out schedules— so many drivers taking their wives and families on holiday.'

Shane looked down at himself with amusement. 'I could change and take my suit with me.' He looked at Anona. 'I'd go if you'd come with me.'

'Look, Shane,' said Spencer, agitated now, 'you can't give me help with one hand and take it away with the other. I'm in a spot with Alfie going off sick.'

'Okay.' Shane smiled. 'Anyway, I wouldn't get there in time with a load trailing behind my back instead of a fast car under my feet. Not to mention with my girl beside me making me forget the time.'

He kissed her again and she clung to the broad shoulders, uncaring that the other man was present. 'Be back soon,' she whispered. The door closed noisily.

'Will you miss me?' Shane murmured against her lips.

'All the time you'll be with me in my thoughts,' she told him. 'And here.' She pressed herself in the region of her heart. His hand pushed hers away, then slipped upwards to possess her breast, pulling her to him. Moments later he was on his way and Anona was left staring after him.

When Anona arrived home after work, she found that her father was not alone. May Howton was with him.

Hearing Anona's turning key, the woman must have gone into the hall. She was robust-looking, her hair tinted and carefully tended, her face pink and round.

Her right hand came out, taking Anona's. She smiled warmly. 'My dear, how nice to meet you. I stayed on especially to make your acquaintance.'

As her right hand returned to her side, Anona noticed that on her left hand she wore a wedding ring, which answered the query in her mind. 'That was kind of you,' Anona remarked, closing the front door and knowing instinctively that she was going to like May Howton.

Anona led the way into the living-room. Her father was looking up at her expectantly and smiled as he saw what he had been searching for. 'I knew you'd like May,' he said, simply.

May added, 'We've got on so well together, your father and I. *And* we've got through quite a lot of work.' She pulled on her jacket which had been draped across a chair. 'I must get back to my little house and cook myself a meal.'

'Can I give you a lift?' Anona offered.

'No car for me, thanks,' May answered firmly. 'I cycle everywhere. It keeps me fit and costs me very little, if anything. But thanks, all the same.' To Will she said, 'I'll be here in the morning.' Will nodded. As May opened the front door she turned to Anona. 'I hope you got on well, too. I also hear you're newly engaged. Congratulations. It's a lovely time, being engaged.' With a lift of her hand she was away, pushing her bicycle down the garden path.

Will said, as Anona returned. 'A very satisfactory day. And a very good choice of assistant. I must ring Morris and thank him for his suggestion.'

Her father's smile was for himself alone. Already, Anona felt, she was being shut out of her father's life. Then she thought of Shane and her future with him. Her father would come and share the Brodie house. His friendship with Morris would fill his leisure hours and May Howton would give him all the help he needed in his work.

It was while they were listening to music that evening that the telephone rang. Anona's heart beat wildly as she lifted the receiver.

'Anona?' Shane's voice was deep and stirred profound longings within her. 'How's my girl?'

'I'm fine.' She smiled, her eyes dancing. 'How's my man?'

There was a deep-throated laughter from the other end. 'Galvanised to life at the sound of you. My God, girl, if you were within touching distance right now, there'd be one hell of a seduction scene and nothing short of the earth shooting off on a space voyage of its own would save you from my lecherous intentions!'

'Do you know,' she answered, her smile persisting, 'I'm beginning to wish there weren't so many miles between ...' There was a hungry growl from the other end and she laughed, saying, 'It's so good to hear you, darling.'

'Is it?' he said, with a tinge of mockery. 'Maybe you like me better at a distance?'

'You know I'd——' If only the telephone were in a more private place! 'I'd rather have you near.'

'How near? So near there's not even room for an air pocket between us?'

'Very near,' was all she could say, knowing that, over the sound of the music which seemed to have been turned down, everything she said could be heard by her father.

There was an unnerving silence from the other end. After her joyous outburst of welcome on hearing his voice, she had become self-conscious and uncomfortable. At least her father had not been able to hear Shane's replies.

'Where——' she cleared her throat. 'Where are you staying, Shane?'

'Where I usually stay—in style at a very good hotel in Central London.'

'Are you—are you alone?' As soon as she had spoken the words, she regretted them.

'At the moment, yes. Why, did you expect me to have rung already for the services of a call-girl?' Anona remained silent. She supposed she had asked for the sarcastic answer. 'It's a little early, don't you think? Another hour or so and I might feel—lonely, mm?'

Her colour flared and she snapped, 'Shane Brodie, I'll see you in——'

'No, you won't, darling. You'll see me in Derbyshire just as soon as I can make it back. Does that please you?'

A deliberately long pause on her part, then a brief, 'Yes.'

A short silence preceded his next question. 'What's wrong with you? Why so inhibited suddenly? It's not your usual line. Whenever I kiss you you're only too happy to——

shall we say—let me share your inner fires. Not to mention almost burn myself in their heat.'

If he was provoking her with his cynicism, there was no way in which she could retaliate. He was not there to see the colour in her cheeks, nor the brightness, like reflected flames, in her eyes. All she could say was, 'Shane, please . . .'

There was a whisper of a wheelchair and out of the corner of her eye, she saw her father turning from the doorway. She was glad she had not spoken her thoughts. Had she done so, her father would have heard her saying, 'Shane, if you were here, my arms would be round you and my mouth would be clinging to yours.'

The silence was broken by Shane's abrupt question, 'Are you being overheard?' Her whispered 'yes' must have reached him. 'For God's sake, Anona, does it matter? He's got to accept me some time. Unless when we're married and I'm his son-in-law, he intends to throw me out every time we go together to see him?'

In despair Anona answered, 'It's just one of those things, Shane. It's not really you, it's because you're effectively the head of the company. That's what I think it is, anyway. How can he have a personal grudge against you?' How could she continue, knowing that every word was being monitored by the man of whom they were talking?

'My father also belongs to the Brodie family,' Shane countered, 'yet your father bears him no grudge.'

'Oh, Shane,' her voice wavered, 'please don't let's quarrel. I love you. If you don't love me, just say so and we'll split up before there's any more damage done.'

'Of course I love you, you silly b——' He caught himself in time. 'Just try and break our engagement and see what happens.'

The receiver was slammed down and Anona was left with a bland, maddeningly neutral burring sound in her ear.

CHAPTER NINE

'So you're Shane's latest.' Anona was sitting at her desk when the newcomer entered.

The woman was tending to plumpness and was dressed in light brown blouse and dark brown skirt. Her appearance benefited from neither item of clothing, although the fact did not seem to worry her.

Anona smiled uncertainly, partly because she did not know the identity of the woman and partly because her words had undoubtedly been spoken to extract further information.

'I'm Elsa,' the woman said, 'Rob's wife.' Her hand stayed at her side. 'You're not his usual type. His women tend more to the flamboyant. I wonder how long he'll wear you in his buttonhole.'

Anger stirred Anona to answer sharply, 'We're engaged.'

'Mm,' said Elsa, 'so I heard.' She turned away, then turned back. 'I wish you luck. You'll need it. And sharp claws—to keep the she-cats at bay, not to mention Shane from straying.'

Rob's wife—nothing to look at, Morris, her father-in-law, had said, but makes up for it with intelligence and common sense. He would not, of course, know of her bitterness, an emotion which so often overrode common sense, where his other son was concerned. Could that bitterness hide admiration? Would Elsa once have liked to have been one of Shane's 'women', but had settled for Rob, the younger brother, as the next best thing?

Or were Elsa's words really spoken with sincerity? Was she trying in her blunt way to warn the girl who, having taken seriously Shane's proposal of marriage, now regarded herself as his fiancée?

132

'I do happen to love Shane,' Anona answered patiently. 'I hope it shows enough to keep him by me and to stop other women from trespassing. But thanks for the advice, Elsa, although I doubt if I'll need it.'

Elsa looked at her and her shrewdness showed. 'Come to think of it,' she commented, 'it might be Shane who'll need that luck.'

Anona smiled. 'If that's a compliment——'

'It was intended that way.'

'Then thanks.'

Elsa appeared about to say more. Instead she shrugged and went away.

There was so much to do, the day passed surprisingly fast. There were so many questions to be answered by telephone. To provide those answers, Anona had to ask others' advice. Drivers returning with empty trucks and reporting faults were asked to take the trucks to the repair depot behind the filling station. There, the trucks would be repaired and made roadworthy again.

When Anona reached home May was there to greet her. 'I'm staying to supper,' she told Anona. 'By invitation from your father. Is it all right with you?'

'Nothing would please me more,' Anona assured her. She did not add, Except for Shane joining us.

With May's help Anona prepared the food. How easily conversation came, Anona thought, with a woman as pleasant as her father's new assistant. It was unbelievable how neatly everything had fallen into place since the moment she and Shane had become engaged. Unbelievable but true—wasn't it?

After May had gone, Will suggested that they might listen to some more music. Anona selected a record by one of his favourite composers. It was while they listened that the anxiety began to gnaw at her—anxiety that the telephone call she had so confidently expected all evening might not come.

Doubt infiltrated the rise and fall of chords and cadences,

making them harsh and dissonant. The uncertainty increased that, even if she waited until midnight, the call from Shane wouldn't come.

Having sat tiredly in the living-room for a long time after her father had gone to bed, Anona finally resigned herself to the fact that she would not hear from Shane that day. Numb and weary with waiting, she undressed and washed.

As she lay in bed, she cried a little inside. Was Elsa right after all? Instead of being Shane's wife-to-be, was she merely just a temporary 'flower in his buttonhole'? And when she faded, would he throw her away?

Anona had expected to be welcomed home by May Howton at the end of each day. She had, in fact, begun to look forward to the woman's warm greeting. Somehow May acted as a mental link between herself and her father.

Since her engagement, the strain in the atmosphere when Anona had been alone in her father's company had been undeniable. The situation upset her, but Will Willis never openly quarrelled with anyone, especially the daughter he loved. So the tension tended to build up instead of being quickly dispersed by an explosive clash which, by its very force, helped to clear the air.

That evening, May stayed on an hour or two. 'You don't mind?' she asked Anona, as they washed and dried the dishes in the kitchen.

'I'm glad, May. I can talk to you.' She placed a dish carefully on the drying rack. 'You're—well, sympathetic and understanding.'

'And your father isn't?'

'Not like you, but then I don't really expect him to be. I suppose,' with a sigh, 'I miss my mother. That doesn't mean,' she added hastily, 'that I'm not fond of my father.'

'I know what you mean. When you talk to him, it's like dragging a ship's anchor from the sea bed.'

Anona laughed. 'He's always absorbed in his own

thoughts. After all, archaeology was—still is—his life's work. He listens patiently enough when I talk to him about my work at Brodie's and so on, but as soon as I stop talking, his head's back in the newspaper or a book.'

'Well, dear,' said May, 'now I'm around, feel free to talk to me whenever you want.' She hung the drying-up towel on the rail. 'I'll sit with your father for a bit.'

Anona glanced at her watch. 'May, I——' She took a deep breath, feeling her heartbeats already increasing at the thought which had lodged itself in her mind. 'I was thinking of going out for a—a short drive.'

May looked outside. 'Lovely evening for it, too. I'll keep your father company. Don't worry about that.'

Anona felt like hugging her. Instead, she rested her hand lightly on May's forearm, then raced along to the living-room. 'Won't be long, Father,' she said.

He nodded, raising his eyes from his book, his spectacles halfway down his nose.

When Anona arrived at Brodie's filling station, she went through the motions of refuelling her petrol tank. Then she drove the car to one side and parked it.

Rob was at the cash desk. A weekly magazine was open on the counter and he was absorbed in its contents. As the shop door opened he looked up, expecting a customer. When he saw that the customer was Anona, a closed expression took possession of his face.

'You don't look very pleased to see me,' she said, with forced lightness. She paid in cash and Rob passed the change across to her.

'You're imagining things.' He pushed around a pile of car stickers. 'How's life treating you? Missing your loved one?'

'Very much. Don't you miss your wife when she's away?'

It seemed she had said the wrong thing. What kind of marriage was it between Rob and Elsa?

'She never goes away.' He spoke in a dead voice.

Did the statement have a double meaning? Anona was

not at that moment bothered enough to delve into other people's problems. All she was aware of was that her heart was behaving madly.

'Rob,' she smiled, 'mind if I use your phone?'

He looked into her pink-cheeked face, gazing momentarily and with a strange malevolence into her bright eyes. 'Blue-eyed blonde,' he said in a spiteful voice. 'Got everything, you have. Trust dear brother Shane to pick out the juiciest morsel from his menu of females!'

'Thanks for the compliment, even though it's twisted. Elsa told me I was just a flower Shane was wearing on his jacket. Implying, I suppose, that when he's done with me, he'll chuck me away. Yet you've just implied that I'm a permanent fixture in his life.'

'Look, the phone's through there in my office. Help yourself and leave me alone, will you?'

'Sorry you've been troubled,' she said brightly, and half-ran to the back of the shop. She picked up the receiver, extended a finger to dial the number—and stopped. How could she telephone a 'very good hotel in Central London' when she didn't even know the number to dial?

Replacing the receiver, she hurried out of the office and into the shop. Rob was deep in his magazine. It was plain that trade was far from brisk.

'Rob?' He looked up touchily. 'Which hotel does Shane stay at when he's in London?'

The magazine was lowered, a malicious smile stretched Rob's lips. 'Suppose I don't tell you?'

Anona forced her shoulders up and down. 'So you don't tell me. I guess I go home.'

'And wait all those hours for your own phone to ring?' She was silent. 'Did he forget all about you last night? You poor little hard-done-by kid!' His sarcasm seemed to be the only characteristic he had in common with his elder brother. Holding her head straight, Anona started to walk to the door.

'Okay. It's the Royal Swan. Heard of it?'

Anona nodded. 'Only because the rich and the famous stay there when they visit this country.'

'Your fiancé has expensive tastes.' His head lowered to read, then lifted. 'Except in the kind of girl he chooses to be his wife. Sensible man. He'll give his wife his pennies, and he'll give his women cheques, fat ones, for their services to——'

'Charity,' she broke in. 'What turned you so sour, Rob? Personally, I think your wife's too good for you.'

She slammed into his office, followed by an expletive and an uncomplimentary description of her ancestry. The local and London directories were in a pile near the telephone. It took three minutes to find the number of the Royal Swan. It took somewhat longer to locate the whereabouts of the man to whom she wanted to speak.

When he said curtly, 'Brodie here,' Anona found herself bordering on the speechless. There was a short exhalation of breath and a smothered, 'What the hell——?'

'Shane,' she managed, 'it's me. Anona.' She could almost hear the broad smile pulling at his lips. He did not answer. Maybe, she thought, it was because she hadn't asked him anything. 'You didn't call last night.' Her voice rose slightly, making the statement into a question.

'No.'

'Were you busy? Is that why——?'

'Very busy.'

She knew she had brought another smile to his face. 'Who was she, Shane? Lidia Harmon-Park?' She could not blunt the edge to her voice.

'Now that would be telling, my sweet.'

'So I guessed right.' Her heart thumped, her breath came quickly.

'Did I say so?' he answered coolly.

'Stop playing with me, Shane!' The angry tearfulness had its way. 'I waited up for hours thinking you'd call me. You let me down. Because you were with another woman. Are we supposed to be engaged or not?' There was no answer. 'All right, *have* your other woman. But you won't keep me dangling, too.' She spoke jerkily. 'No staying power, you said. Well, as I said, I want the man *I* marry to be faithful, so there's no point in our engagement going on.'

'Do you love me?' The question was so unexpected the truth was forced from her.

'Yes, you know I do. Very much.'

'Shouldn't trust and marriage go hand in hand?'

'All right, I'm sorry, but——' He knew she loved him because she had just told him, so why shouldn't she commit herself to him even further? 'I just wanted to hear your voice.'

'Did you, my love?' he said softly. 'Now you've heard it, how do you feel?'

'It—it does things to me,' she whispered. 'Oh, Shane, when will you be home?'

The brief pause should have warned her of the sarcasm to come. 'Are you pleading with me, my sweet? Are you begging for a man, although you once swore you never would?'

Anona inhaled, exhaled, then said, 'Shane Brodie, I'm putting the phone down on you!'

His mocking laughter made her check the receiver's descent. She couldn't really hang up on the man she loved. He assumed she was still there, because he spoke again. 'You're very free with your verbal love-play this evening. Is your father out?'

'I'm calling from the filling station shop. Rob said it was okay.'

'Brother Rob gave his kind permission, did he?'

'Yes. Are you annoyed now that the firm's paying for the call?'

'On the contrary, it makes me feel freer to go on talking to my beloved. Do you know what I'm doing, Anona? I'm lying on my bed and imagining you're beside me. My eyes are closed and I can see—no, I'll keep my beautiful visions of you to myself until I see you again tomorrow evening. Am I embarrassing you?'

In the circumstances how could she tell him, My whole body's throbbing with love for you? She heard herself whisper, 'I wish I were in your arms and that you were kissing me until I couldn't think any more.'

Someone came into the shop and she could hear their discussion quite clearly. If she was able to hear them, then Rob had probably heard the whole of her conversation with Shane.

'Request noted, Miss Willis,' said Shane lazily. 'When we meet tomorrow evening, make sure it's private. When I've slipped the engagement ring I've bought you on to your finger, there'll be no limits to my demands on that love you have for me. No limits, you understand?'

Her eyes were sparkling, her voice catching in her throat as she said, 'Shane, I must go. Rob's in there, talking to someone. He must have heard everything I've said.'

'So Rob heard,' he drawled. 'If he hadn't, he'd have made it up.'

'Tomorrow,' said Anona. 'What time, Shane?'

'Eight. At my place.'

'Goodnight, darling,' Anona whispered, but Shane had gone.

Rob was alone when Anona returned to the shop. He was reading his magazine again. He looked up and his eyes moved over her fair-skinned face which was alive with vitality and love for the man to whom she had just been talking.

'So you love him,' Rob commented, 'really love him.'

'Yes, I do,' she answered firmly. 'Is it so strange that I should love the man I'm engaged to?'

Rob studied her for a seemingly endless period of time. From a curiously twisted mouth there came a smile. 'He hasn't told you, then?'

'Told me what?' Her mouth began to grow dry, her heart to beat like a hammer driving in a nail.

The magazine was lowered to the counter. Rob's hands bunched into fists. 'About your father's accident.' A fine film was appearing on Rob's upper lip.

'What about my father's accident?'

'It's a family secret, really.' His spiteful eyes slid over her. 'But since you're soon to be one of the family, I really think you should be told.'

Anona found that her jaws had grown rigid. She managed to say, 'Don't you think you should leave it to Shane to tell me?'

'You're the last person he'd tell.' There was a long agonising silence. Anona did not know whether Rob was tantalising her or whether there was truly a struggle going on within him.

'Well?' Her voice was hoarse.

'Shane was the driver of the truck which knocked your father down.'

Anona swayed, put a shaking hand on the counter to steady herself and stayed like a statue. The door opened, a customer entered. Which was just as well, she thought later, since her mind had blacked out.

The customer went. There was silence. Anona tried to find her voice, her mind started up again like an old car engine spluttering to reluctant life. *So Rob heard*, Shane had said. *If he hadn't, he would have made it up.*

'I don't believe you,' she said.

Rob shrugged. 'Ask Shane.' He picked up the magazine, scanned the pages. 'It's the ghost in the family cupboard.'

'I don't believe you!' Her voice had risen, her brow was damp. Disbelief was her only lifeline now. To that she must cling—at least until she knew the truth. At the door she turned—to catch the malicious smile which had been directed at her back.

'You really do hate your brother, don't you?' Anona challenged.

'Do I?' The answer was noncommittal. 'I'll admit I envy him for everything he's got that I haven't.'

'And do your best to take it from him.'

'You still don't believe what I've told you, do you? Just ask him, then you'll see that what——' He looked beyond her. 'Come in, Jimmy. I saw you driving the truck round the back.'

Anona recognised the man who stood patiently behind her waiting to be let into the shop. She moved, but he said, 'Hi, Miss Willis.'

'Hallo, Jimmy.' She forced her reluctant mind to think of business matters. 'Back from Manchester?'

'Just. Traffic was heavy.'

Her brain was functioning more clearly now. 'I've got a job lined up for you tomorrow. Electrical goods to go to Harwich.'

'Can't do it, Miss Willis. Came back loaded with stuff for Bristol. I'll be off first thing in the morning.'

'But this is a rush job.' To Rob, she said coldly, 'Mind if I phone Spencer?'

With a sweep of his hand, Rob invited her to use his office telephone again. Spencer went through the drivers on their payroll, but found that every one of them was either booked for a journey or away in other parts. 'I'll do it myself,' he said.

'I'd forgotten you could drive a truck.'

'Had to learn when I joined the family firm. I'm one of the family, too, aren't I?'

Anona answered, 'Sorry, I forgot the family rules. Does Rob do truck driving?'

'He had a go, but gave it up, to his father's disgust. But Rob always was the difficult one of the family.'

Anona thought, You can say that again. 'Does that mean,' she asked Spencer, 'that someone else will be in charge of the Traffic Department tomorrow?'

'Yes. You.' He must have heard her swift breath because he said, 'You càn do it, Anona. You know most of it by now. I may be away a couple of days. I think there's an order from a customer to pick up a load at Harwich and bring it back to this area.'

Two days in charge! Anona hoped she wouldn't make a mistake. A reputation for reliability, she had been told, was the most important factor in transport. With Shane's return on her mind, and having to face him with the facts which Rob had told her about her father's accident ... facts? 'He'd make it up,' Shane had said about Rob. And hadn't Rob tried to make trouble between them by telling Shane that she had said they were engaged?

Until she challenged Shane and asked him for the truth, those words of Shane's summing up Rob's character would have to carry her through the difficult hours until his return.

Anona found that running the Traffic Department without Spencer was a demanding business. Even with the help of an assistant, there were some queries she could not answer.

Being so busy had kept her worries at the back of her mind, but at coffee and tea-breaks and mealtimes, as she sat alone in the self-service restaurant, she could not prevent her thoughts from wandering and wondering.

As she drove home and the demands of work receded, a nagging anxiety took command of her mind. Long ago she had begun counting the hours, and then the minutes, to Shane's return. What if Rob had been telling the truth? What if Shane had really run her father down?

May Howton stayed to an evening meal again. She was as at home in the cottage, even after a few days, as Anona was. As she helped Anona prepare the food, she questioned her with sincere interest about how she had coped that day without more senior help. During the meal, May talked just as easily to Will. When she prepared to leave for her own home, Anona felt genuinely sorry.

With her father's head in a book, she was left alone to

think and worry and watch the hands of the clock move inexorably on. She should have been excited, happy, unable to stay still. The tension which stiffened her limbs kept that restlessness and anticipation imprisoned behind mountain-high walls of uneasiness.

At seven-thirty she went to her bedroom to dress. Deciding on simplicity, she chose a scarlet short-sleeved shirt-blouse and a white button-through skirt. Round her neck she fastened a string of white beads and in her ears white earrings. Her wayward hair was parted slightly off-centre, falling in a cascade of curls to her shoulders.

As she descended the stairs, the phone rang. Shane—to cancel?

'Morris here,' came the hearty voice from the other end. 'Is your father available to visitors, love? I wouldn't want to wish myself on him if he didn't want it.'

Will called from the living-room, 'Who's that? Morris? Tell him to come over. He'll keep me company.'

Anona recalled that her father had not been over-pleased when she had told him she would be going out that evening. He had been even less pleased—she could tell by the way his eyes did not stray from his book as she had told him—when he heard it was her fiancé she would be going to see.

'I heard that,' said Morris. 'I'll gladly keep him company. I'm on my way.'

Before Anona could ask whether Shane had yet arrived home, Morris had gone. He came as she was preparing to leave. When she opened the door, Morris lifted a long, strong arm and, placing it across her shoulders, pulled her near enough to kiss her cheek.

'He's waiting, is Shane,' said Morris. 'I could hear him striding about his room like a caged lion waiting for its mate.'

Anona laughed and felt the tension ease away. 'I'm not that yet,' she said.

'Maybe not, but you will be, you will be. Now off you

go. I'll see myself in, no need to do the honours.' As she ran out to her car, Morris called after her, 'I'll stay here till you get back.'

She waved and was away. The evening sun was a great ball of gold setting over the high moors, throwing long black hill-shadows across the green of the grass. Her spirits were as high as those hills, and it was as if she had never been told lies about Shane by his spiteful, envious brother. For of course it was a lie that Shane had driven the truck that had knocked down her father. Hadn't Shane implied that it was Rob's habit to make things up just to stir up trouble?

· But she had to know. It was imperative that she should learn the truth from Shane's own lips. She could not have that doubt hanging over her for the whole of their lives together.

Shane opened the door. He had not yet changed from his business suit. The 'boss' image still hung around him like a clinging mist and Anona wanted to reach out and brush it away. Her blue eyes lifted to his, uncertain yet sure of her welcome. Why shouldn't she be sure?

Seconds before he smiled she had caught in the depth of his gaze a hard, appraising look. Then warmth came with his words of welcome, banishing all doubt from her mind. His arms opened wide and she went into them, and stayed there, cheek against his chest, feeling the thudding of his heart beneath the surface hardness.

His hand felt for her chin and he moved back sufficiently to tilt her chin. A few moments of intense scrutiny of each and every feature, then his mouth came down and she was lost in him. He lifted his head, only to return again for more and yet more, as if he would never satisfy his thirst.

At last he held her away, gripping her hand and pulling her behind him up the stairs to his suite of rooms. They entered the living-room, but he pulled her through the communicating door into his bedroom. Still gripping her hand, he opened a drawer and took out a box. With his thumb he eased open the lid, put the box down and extracted a ring.

He raised her left hand, moved the Blue John stone ring to another finger and eased on the engagement ring. It was a perfect fit.

'Sapphire and diamonds,' he said. 'I remembered the size from the other ring.'

Her eyes sparkled more brightly than the diamonds. 'Shane, it's beautiful! But the cost!'

'What does the cost matter when the girl who's wearing the ring is worth more to me than all the diamonds in the world?'

'Am I?'

'You know the answer to that, my love.'

Her eyes lifted from admiring the ring to watch him remove his jacket. His shirt was striped blue and white, his tie a dark blue. Slowly he rolled up his sleeves and she saw the powerful muscles in his arms, the strong hands, hands which could grip and turn a giant steering wheel ...

Or fail to turn that steering wheel to avoid knocking a man down, crippling that man for life.

As she watched him, so he, hands on hips, watched her. His whole body was a challenge. A thick, black eyebrow arched sardonically.

'Found the courage to ask me yet?'

The question had her gazing at him wide-eyed. His eyes narrowed and she knew then that prevarication would serve no purpose. Somehow he knew that she knew about Rob's allegations and he was challenging her to challenge him. Did it have to be now? she asked herself, distressed. So soon after their reunion, when her whole body ached to be close to his?

Her left hand clenched, as if it made its own decision never to let the ring go, breaking the newly-formed bond. She turned her fist to look at the ring, only half seeing the diamonds glinting in the glow from the evening sun as it flooded in through the windows.

'Courage?' she asked. 'It wasn't courage I needed, Shane. It was——' she looked up, seeing that his eyes had hardened, 'it was the right moment.'

'What's wrong with now?'

'All right.' Her head lifted boldly. 'I can see Rob's told you that he told me about the accident. That you were the Brodie driver who ran my father down and turned him into a permanent invalid.'

'You say it as though you believe it.' He folded his arms and stood, legs apart, his whole attitude belligerent. 'Have you tried me in that little mind of yours, judged me and condemned me without giving me a hearing?'

'Shane!' she cried out, like a lamb that knew it was about to be slaughtered. 'Don't talk like that. Rob told me what he said was the truth. It was a family ghost, he said, and one I ought to know since I was going to be a member of the family. I said I wanted you to tell me yourself because I didn't believe him. He—he said I was the last person you'd tell.'

Shane gazed at her, lips a thin line. Then, to her dismay, he turned from her and went to the window, gazing out at the pleasant gardens bathed in evening gold. Anona looked at his rounded shoulders, watched as a hand moved to rub his forehead.

'Shane,' she whispered, 'it's not true. Is it?'

He did not answer and she ran to him, wrapping her arms about him, pressing her cheek against his back, placing little kisses wherever she could reach above his waist. For a few moments he tolerated her desperate ardour, then, with a muttered oath, pulled at her arms, removing them, swinging her round and by the shoulders forcing her away.

'It's true. Now what are you going to do about it?'

Slowly he walked towards her. She backed away. The colour had drained from her face. He stopped. She stopped.

'Yet all the time,' she accused, her voice choked, 'you let me believe it was someone else. You shrugged your shoulders. To you, my father was just another accident statistic. Knocking him down was simply an unfortunate event which was passed over to your insurance company.'

'He admitted liability. You've known all the time that he was in the wrong. There were witnesses to prove it. He had no case.'

'All right, I accept all that.' The tears were rising. She forced them back. 'It's your attitude that gets me, your—your dishonesty in not telling me.'

'That I happened to be at the wheel when the truck knocked your father down? Would it have made any difference to what followed? To us?'

'Yes, yes. Oh, can't you see? I couldn't marry a man who did that to my father. Not only would I feel repulsion for him—my father bears that man a lifelong grudge. He'll never accept you as a son-in-law now. And I'll never leave him.'

Shane began to move towards her again. Once more she backed away, a curious fear growing inside her. His head was down slightly. His hands were working at his tie, loosening it, discarding it, unfastening his shirt buttons.

'Do I repel you?' he asked softly. 'Now you know what you know, does the thought of my hands touching you make you cringe? Hands that steered straight at your father?'

'Stop it!' she cried, her eyes brimming.

He was a different man, frightening yet magnetic. She wanted to run away, she wanted to run towards him. She came up against a piece of furniture, a wardrobe door was hard behind her back. Then he was there in front of her, pressing his length against hers. His arms crushed her against him and left her fighting for breath.

'I told you on the phone that once my ring was on your finger, there'd be no limits to my demands on you. You're wearing my ring, so I'll keep my promise.' His teeth snapped together, his hands clamped on to her shoulders and he shook her until she was choked with exhaustion and fear.

He was angry, angry with *her*! Why, she thought through

the mist that was closing in, why with her? It was he who had committed the crime, not she. How could she be blamed for rejecting him now that she knew the truth, now she knew how dishonest he was?

He lifted her and carried her, coping easily with her struggles. Then the softness of the bed was beneath her and he was beside her, his hand at her blouse buttons. She tried to stop him, but his hand was as unyielding to her scraping nails as his jaw was to her pleas for him to stop.

When he jerked her blouse from her shoulders and she felt his hand seeking and finding with indisputable possession the curving softness of her breasts, when his lips fastened ruthlessly over hers and drained from her all impulse to resist, she let herself slide into the mist that had been clouding her mind almost from the moment of their reunion.

'I'll have you,' he said thickly, trailing her throat, her ear, her swollen lips. 'I'll claim that innocence that looks from those blue, trusting eyes. I'll make you mine so completely that any man who comes after will leave you cold.'

His mouth was brutal, his hands were savage and bruising, inflicting on her the pain it seemed she had inflicted on him. The heat of his desires put a match to her passion until it roared in her ears, deafening her to all whispers of caution.

She was lost in the love she felt for him, wanting to be enfolded in him, yielding to the pressure of his hips against hers, his exploring lips, his caressing, gripping hands. There was an overpowering wish in her mind and body to give him the pleasure and the satisfaction he craved from her, no matter how harshly he was treating her.

As she fought, gasping, through the haze to reach the neutral ground of relative sanity, she knew the time was not far off when her body would yield to him of its own accord —unless her reason prevailed and her words could persuade him back to rationality.

In desperation she moved beneath him, but had to acknowledge that his strength was so great in comparison with hers he might not even have noticed. She made herself go rigid, forcing all her limbs to repel him, but the action only served to increase his determination to make her his.

In the face of her weakness against his strength, she knew that the inevitable was near. Involuntarily she began to sob, great spasms shook her, telling of her wretchedness and despair. Tears welled and overflowed, moistening his pillow, running down her cheeks until she could taste the salt.

Shane must have tasted it, too, because he lifted his head. In the half-light he looked satanic, his long sweep of jaw relentless, a muscle working in his cheek. He rolled away to lie beside her, still—so still she became afraid. He was staring at the ceiling.

'So I repel you. I stand condemned.' His sarcasm in such circumstances hurt like a physical assault.

Slowly Anona pulled off his sapphire and diamond ring, placing it on his scarcely-moving chest. He picked it up and flung it on to the bedside rug. She shifted, rolling over face downwards, and let the hopeless tears come.

He got up, smoothed his hair, rebuttoned his shirt and walked to the window, tying his tie. At the door he turned.

'You'd better go. I don't want a woman as my wife who has no trust in me.'

She rolled on to her back, gripping together the edges of her opened blouse. 'How can I trust you?' she cried. 'You've admitted it's true.'

He gave her a long, hard look and went out. There was, of course, no answer he could give. It was the end of their relationship. They could not even be friends any more, let alone lovers.

For some time Anona lay still, limp with unhappiness, scarcely able to grasp what had happened. The mists were clearing, allowing her mind to function with painful clarity. Would Shane, she wondered, still allow her to work for

Brodie's? Would Morris stop visiting her father, thus depriving him of something he had come to enjoy?

When it came to her that she was lying, not on her own bed but Shane's, she got up, finding her sandals which had fallen off as Shane had carried her, protesting, to his bed. Looking in the mirror, she blushed at the dishevelled state of her hair and her clothing.

A comb lay on the dressing-table. She ran its long black teeth through her hair, fluffing out the curls to frame her face. The door opened and, dropping the comb, she turned, leaning defensively against the dressing-table top. Shane's eyes dropped lazily to her blouse and all that was revealed beneath it. Quickly her fingers lifted to close the gap. She had forgotten to fasten the buttons!

'Wanting more?' Shane drawled. 'Were you waiting for me to return and join you again on the bed?'

Anona could have said, I was too stunned to move. It took me time to find enough energy. She decided, however, to stay silent, turning to the mirror and picking up the comb again.

'I hope you don't object to my using this?' she asked his reflection which stood, hands pocketed, leaning indolently against the door and watching her.

'I shower every day, which means my hair's clean, so the comb is fit for a queen, let alone you.' The last three words contained a trace of contempt.

Tidy now, she turned. 'Why are you in here?'

'It's my bedroom. I think I'm entitled to ask you that.'

'You brought me here.'

'For love.'

'Which turned to hate.'

At the barb, his eyes narrowed. 'It did, didn't it? Since you haven't had the sense to get out while I let you, I could lock this door and do what the hell I liked with you.' He came towards her. She willed herself to stay where she was.

His hands gripped her arms, fingertips pressing in, bruising her flesh. She winced but closed her mouth on a cry.

'What's wrong?' he snarled. 'Don't you like my touch any more? Do you feel defiled now you know it was my hands that caused your father's accident?'

She said, her lips hardly moving with pain, 'You're hurting me, Shane.' Only when a tearless sob shook her did he relax his grip. She would carry his bruises for days, she thought, which would be all that was left of their love. If there had, on his part, ever been any love.

'I'll take you back,' he said.

'I'll take myself. My car's here.'

He shook his head. 'I contacted Jim. He came over ten minutes ago and took it back to your home. He's walking back. When I return you, I'll pick up my father. Talking of my father,' he strolled to the window, 'I have a request to make.' Anona was silent and waiting. 'He's so happy about this engagement of ours it would come as a bad shock to him to hear that it lasted only four days. A shock in his state of health could be a disaster.'

Anona studied the broad, masculine back across the room, the mere sight of the latent strength in his shoulders and hips stirring in her feelings that disturbed and aroused. She wished she didn't love the man who so plainly did not love her back, despite his statement to the contrary.

The engagement ring still lay where it had been thrown. She studied it abstractedly, saying, 'You're not asking me to go on pretending we're engaged?'

Shane turned and rested his hips against the low sill. His pants were well-fitting, moulding to his thighs, bringing to life inside her a longing to be impelled against his body and kissed into oblivion.

He appeared to guess her thoughts, for a sardonic smile played over his mouth. 'I am. Would it be so terrible? You don't exactly object to my lovemaking. If I were to lift my finger right now and beckon, you'd cross that distance between us in a few seconds.'

'Yes,' she hit back, 'I'd cross that space by throwing

something at you. And what's more, I'd make darned sure it landed right on target!'

She swung away, smoothing her skirt, and found to her dismay that in his lovemaking on the bed he had unfastened some of the lower buttons. He must have seen her embarrassment because she heard a low laugh from behind her.

'Were you so carried away you didn't even know where my hands were wandering?'

Exasperated, she faced him and exclaimed, 'Oh, you—you——'

'Well, what's your answer? Are you a good enough actress to carry it through convincingly?'

'For how long?'

He shrugged and strolled towards her. 'Believe me, my love,' he said caustically, 'no longer than is absolutely necessary. My needs as a man are persistent in their demands to be satisfied—as you're beginning to learn—and going around in close contact with an unresponsive, ice-bound woman is not something I'm greatly looking forward to.'

She wanted to shout at him that, as he knew very well, she was by nature warm and loving. All her love and all her life would be his, if only he hadn't been the one who had driven that truck at her father.

'There's always Lidia Harmon-Park for you to fall back on,' she hit out.

'Ah, yes,' he pulled on his jacket, 'Lidia certainly has her uses. But not to fall *back* on, my love. Surely you know your elementary human biology?'

Anona drew a breath through her teeth. 'You—you make me sick, Shane Brodie!' Her hand lifted, swung—and was caught in a relentless grip. With his free hand he jerked her against him, forcing back her head under the brutality of his kiss. The kiss lasted so long, deepening in its demands, that she was forced to cling to him, thinking, In a moment I'll faint ... I can't stand the pain ... I can't even breathe.

When he let her go, she was forced to bend double, holding her head, to prevent that faint. Arms folded, Shane watched, offering no help, smiling in a cruel way. As she straightened at last, he said quietly,

'Now I think you'd better pick up that ring. You'll need to wear it for a while.'

'You pick it up. You threw it there.'

Her defiance narrowed his eyes. 'I'm waiting.'

With immense reluctance she obeyed, handing the ring to him, but it seemed he had not yet finished humiliating her. He shook his head. 'This is just a false engagement. You must put it on.'

'I've a good mind to throw——'

'Take my advice, my lovely—control your baser instincts, otherwise I'll show you some of mine.'

Forcing the ring on to her engagement finger, she snapped, 'It's a good thing I've found you out at last! Now I know your real character, you rotten, low-down near-murderer——'

His hand lifted and found its target before she knew he had moved. She staggered under the impact. Her cheek stung so much her lips trembled and her eyes overflowed. She swung away, hand to the redness. After a long, throbbing pause she said, 'I'm sorry.'

Shane went to the door. 'I'll drive my car round to the front. Join me there.'

CHAPTER TEN

It was the days that followed that were to prove the hardest to endure. Although Anona's work was in the Traffic Department of Brodie's, it shared the same building as the main office, which meant that she often saw Shane and heard his voice.

If they passed in a corridor and others were around, he would smile at her, although his eyes remained blank. He might even stop her and place a fleeting kiss on her lips. If he did, she would immediately draw them in as if to emphasise that they were her property, not his. If they met and they were alone, Shane would barely look at her, treating her as if she were an ordinary employee.

Towards the end of the first week, Shane called Anona to his office. He invited her impersonally to sit down, remaining standing himself. 'It's not enough,' he told her. 'My father's growing restive. He keeps asking why we're not seeing each other in our spare time. Has your father noticed?'

She shook her head. 'May Howton stays on for a long time these days. It's almost as if he's encouraging her, and preparing himself for the day I get married and leave.'

Shane tapped the desk with a pencil. 'Is May happy about staying on, extending her duties? Does she show any irritation, for instance?'

'On the contrary, she seems only too glad. They get on so well together.' Even she had noticed the unconscious note of wistfulness which had crept in as she had spoken. 'In fact, I'm wondering whether . . .' Her voice tailed off, unwilling to speak her thoughts to this man who would soon have been her husband, if only—— She put a brake on her mind. Those two words never did anyone any good.

154

'Wouldn't it be a good thing if they married one day?' He had intercepted the wistfulness and brought it into the open. Wonderful, she was thinking, if you and I were still going to be married. She nodded and he asked, 'What will you do?'

He was cold and indifferent about her future, which showed how false his claim to have loved her had been.

'Move out,' she said carelessly. 'Find a job.'

'You've got a job. Here, at Brodie's.'

Work on at Brodie's, seeing Shane every day, passing him unacknowledged once their fake engagement had ended, being treated as of less importance than that pencil he had tossed on to his desk?

'I wouldn't stay here, thank you.' She hoped the disdain in her voice would reach him. By the hardening of his eyes, it had.

'For this arrangement between us to be convincing, we've got to be together more often. This evening I'll take you to dinner somewhere.'

Her heart leapt, only to fall calamitously on the other side of the fence. For show, that's all it would be. 'If you wish,' she said tonelessly.

'I'll call for you at seven and book a table for seven-forty-five.'

When Shane arrived, May Howton had not left. 'He's here,' she called upstairs to Anona. 'I'll stay until you come back. No, I don't mind at all. And I don't think your father wants to get rid of me yet,' she added jokingly.

'On the contrary,' Will called from the living-room. 'I welcome your company.'

As Anona came down, May let Shane in. After he had greeted May, his eyes lifted, noting Anona's rose-pink sleeveless summer dress which matched the rising colour in her cheeks. His gaze flicked over her shape and young, fresh lines which were not hidden by the close-fitting dress. For a moment his expression did not alter, then he seemed to remember his role.

His hand came out and as she placed hers in it, he pulled her to him. Perversely she kept her head down until he was forced to ask, 'A kiss, my darling?' But the request was accompanied by angry pressure on her fingers.

Tilting her head but refusing to stand on tiptoe, she made him bend for that kiss. The quick smile she gave him was mischievous and she saw his jaw move ominously. May looked on with indulgence.

'Make the most of these waiting days,' she told them gently. 'Young people nowadays don't know what they're missing in taking everything all at once. I wouldn't be young these days for a fortune!'

They had moved into the living-room to join Will. After a nod at Shane and a glance at the joined hands, Will said to May, 'I'm sure you're lying, my dear. Be honest and admit you'd love to have your youth over again.'

She considered the question, shook her head, then went on, 'But that's a matter for talking about another time. I find it good just to look at these two young people. Have you seen such happiness?'

Surely, Anona thought, my feelings can't be as transparent as that! And Shane? She looked up at him. His eyes were shining down into hers. Who had taught him to act so well? No doubt he was thinking the same of her.

Her father's gaze rested on her for a few seconds, then moved upward to her companion. A strange expression came into Will's eyes—was it questioning, analysing? It was the same look as they used to hold in the old days when he had examined broken relics from the past, trying to piece them together.

The drive through the valleys and over the moorland heights was so breathtaking that speech was unnecessary. Which was just as well, Anona mused, her heart heavy. Shane was certainly in no mood for talking. Where was that look of love he had simulated so well in front of her father and May Howton? Where, too, had her own happiness gone in just being with him?

By the time they reached the restaurant her appetite had faded. The drink which Shane had ordered for her as they waited to be called to their table revived it sufficiently for her to eat most of the food that was put in front of her, but in the face of Shane's uncompromising silence, she did not enjoy the meal.

Towards the end he said, 'We shall have to meet again tomorrow.' She nodded. 'I don't know about you,' he said, 'but I'm finding this pretence at happiness too much of a strain.'

'I only agreed to it for your sake.'

'Am I denying that?'

Her gaze shifted from his, finding escape by carefully replacing her coffee cup on the saucer.

'What do you suggest we do?' she asked dully.

'I'll come for you again in the evening and take it from there.' He called for the bill and settled it. 'I'll be away at a meeting most of the day.' They were walking towards the exit, her jacket swinging from her shoulders.

'Good,' she responded, goaded to anger by his detachment. 'That means I won't have to meet you in passing, forcing myself to smile at you.'

'In two minutes from now,' he said through his teeth, 'you'll be across my knee and I'll be hitting you hard where it hurts!'

'Just like you hit my father.' The words were out before she knew her lips were saying them.

'I've changed my mind,' he gritted, unlocking the car. 'I'll get hold of you,' his eyes slid upwards to her throat, smooth and inviting in the light of the car park lamps, 'in a much more dangerous place.'

Anona turned and walked away. In a few strides Shane was beside her, gripping her arm and turning her back to the car. 'Stop *talking* to me like that!' she choked, her throat tight with tears.

'Yes, I wondered how long you could fence with me before you crumpled verbally at my feet.'

'Take me home,' she told him, slamming the passenger door, 'just take me home.'

He did, without speaking another word.

'I didn't mean to play Peeping Tom just now,' said May Howton, opening the door to Anona.

'I didn't even see you,' Anona answered lightly, pulling off her jacket. Thank goodness her face was flushed from Shane's goodnight kiss. It had been forced on them by the lifted curtain which Shane had noticed as Anona had prepared to get out of the car.

'We'd better part in the usual way expected of an engaged couple,' Shane had said. 'May's looking.'

His kiss had been far more thorough than had been necessary and she had not dared to struggle against him. When his face lifted, the sardonic grin that greeted her stormy eyes had made her want to hit out. She grasped his tie and pulled.

Instead of resisting as she had judged he would, he had come with it, his mouth descending again to cover hers. He was laughing this time. 'See you tomorrow,' he had said lazily, watching her go.

'Only for your father's sake!' was her sharp retort as she swung along the garden path.

Shane called out to her the following morning as she walked along the corridor with Spencer, 'Remember this evening.' Anona had forced a smile and waved.

'He's got it badly,' Spencer commented with a smile. 'I've never known Shane be so taken with a woman before. What have you got that all the others haven't? No, don't tell me,' he had smiled broadly, 'I'll tell you. There isn't a carbon copy of you anywhere around, is there? I wouldn't mind a girl out of your mould myself.'

'No sister,' Anona said, laughing. 'Sorry about that.'

'The sorrow's all mine,' Spencer answered as they went their separate ways.

That evening, when Shane called for Anona, he drew up

at the curb outside the cottage and hooted. 'Why doesn't he come in?' Will asked, a little petulantly. Anona was surprised by the question. Did he want to get to know a little better the man he assumed would soon become his son-in-law?

'I'm ready to go,' she replied. 'Look!" She twirled round, forcing a gaiety she did not feel at the thought of another evening spent in Shane's company. Her father accepted her explanation and went back to his book. 'The Pattersons will bring you in some coffee soon,' she told him.

'Don't know why May couldn't have stayed on,' he grumbled.

Again Anona was surprised. 'She was going to a bridge party. She told you, Father.'

'I could have gone with her. I may have lost the use of my legs, but my brain's still functioning well, not to mention my hands.'

The hooting was repeated and Anona said, exasperated with her father, her pretend fiancé, May Howton, everybody, 'If you'd told her you were interested, I'm sure she would have invited you.'

'You'd better go,' Will remarked with a sigh. 'That young man out there's as impatient as they come. Worse than I am, from the sound of it, and I thought I was bad enough!'

Anona laughed as she dashed down the steps to the gate. The laughter lingered on her lips and in her eyes as she got into the car. Shane looked her over quizzically. 'Excited by the prospect of passing yet another boring evening with the man you agreed to marry, then chucked his ring back at him?'

'I was laughing at something my father said,' she told him firmly, hoping she had put him in his place. 'About you.'

If she had thought the matter would end there, she was mistaken. 'Oh?' Shane queried. 'What about me?'

'He said you're impatient. Worse than he is, in fact.'

'He's right.' Shane's voice sounded grim. They moved from the curb and began their journey. 'Especially with stupid, blue-eyed, fair-haired young women who can't see beyond the ends of their noses.'

'What's that supposed to mean?' He was silent. 'Are you trying to pick a quarrel?'

He did not bother to answer.

'Where are we going?' She seemed always to be asking him that question these days.

'To my home. Where else? My father's going out to some friends.'

So they would be alone. Anona did not know whether to be pleased or anxious. The feeling between them was anything but easy. Even there, in the car, her awareness of him was increasing by the minute. Watching his hands on the wheel, glancing at his powerful thighs and remembering his skill in controlling the great truck in which he had given her a lift when they had first met, had the blood swirling around her body before the evening had even begun.

The car swung into the drive of his house and Anona let herself out. As she waited for Shane to lock the car and find his house key, the front door was opened.

'Welcome in,' said Morris, his tall figure filling the doorway. 'Come in, my dear. Make yourself comfortable. This'll be your home soon, won't it, eh?'

Anona hated deceiving this big, warm-hearted man. She reached up spontaneously to kiss his cheek and his face glowed. 'My, you're going to make a fine daughter-in-law! You've chosen well, son. You took your time making up your mind, but when you did, you couldn't have picked a finer wife for yourself.'

Uncertainly, Anona glanced back at Shane. His face was expressionless.

'I thought you were going to visit friends,' said Shane.

Morris shook his head. 'Felt a bit off-colour. Nothing wrong, mind, but thought an evening watching the television would be better for me.'

Anona saw an opportunity to bypass the time she had dreaded spending alone with Shane. 'May we join you?' she asked, sitting down and settling herself as if she were prepared to spend the whole evening and night there if necessary.

A quick glance at Shane told her of his annoyance. Impishly she patted the chair next to hers. 'Come and join me, darling,' she invited.

Morris sat in his favourite seat. Shane removed his jacket. 'With pleasure, my love,' he said, going across to her. Instead of sitting in the chair she had indicated, he bent and scooped her up, took her place in the chair and sat her on his knee.

She was caught and he knew it. He grinned down into her face, so near to his, and placed a swift kiss on her protesting, parted lips. There was nothing she could say, no way in which she could show her anger without upsetting Morris, and that was something which on no account did she want to do.

Through the television film they were watching there was a chance to escape from unhappy reality and she could let herself believe that she and Shane were really soon to be married.

Her head lowered to Shane's chest, a contented sigh escaped her and he shifted his arms which were around her to make her more comfortable. Soon other feelings started to creep in. The close contact with his body, plus her own desires reaching out from their hiding place waiting to be discovered, had a restlessness seeping through her.

It was impossible to keep still. She began to fidget as the conviction grew that, in the circumstances, she should not be lying in Shane's arms, that he had no right to lift her from the chair and put her on to his lap. It was really overdoing the pretence. Why couldn't he have sat in another chair and just smiled at her now and then? That would have satisfied his father as much as what he had chosen to do.

It was, of course, an act which was intended to annoy her. If only she had thought of that before, she wouldn't now be lying here so submissively! Her restlessness increased and, making sure that Morris was absorbed in the film, she directed her eyes upwards to try to convey to Shane how irritated she was growing at his forcing her to stay there.

By the tightening of his arms into a grip of steel, she knew that he was warning her—'Be still or my father will notice.' Angry now, she stretched upward and whispered in his ear, 'Shane, let me go!'

Shane whispered back, 'You're staying right here until I've finished with you,' which statement, of course, only angered her more.

There was a low rumble of laughter shaking Morris's large frame, but his eyes did not stray from the film. When, five minutes later, it was over he rose, stretched and said, 'I think I'll be off to bed.'

Shane, concerned at once, asked, 'Something wrong?'

'Not really, lad. Just tired. And,' with a smiling glance at them, 'you don't want an old man like me sitting here when all you two really want to do is have a good cuddle.'

Anona struggled to sit up, but Shane held her back. 'Please, Mr Brodie, don't go because of us. We'll——'

Morris's hand lifted. 'I'm off upstairs. See you in the morning, son.'

As soon as there was the sound of a bedroom door closing, their eyes met. Anona shivered inside at the sudden coldness she encountered.

'You're free,' said Shane. 'No audience now to act to, although I must admit I found your acting superb.'

Gasping at his effrontery, she snapped, 'You can talk! You could get yourself a part in a film any day.'

'Are you moving,' he asked coldly, 'or am I going to have to tip you off my lap?'

Indignantly, Anona struggled away from him to stand on

the hearthrug. 'I want to go home,' she said. 'Will you please take me?'

Shane stretched out his long legs, lifting his arms to cushion his head. 'When I'm ready.'

'All right, I'll walk.' She went to the door.

'You go when I say and not before.' His tone held an underlying authority she could not ignore, but she still hesitated, undecided as to whether or not to defy him.

His eyes came open. They were cool and utterly impartial and she wanted to throw herself on top of him, battering him and crying, Why? Why did it have to be you of all people who knocked my father down? I love you, I'll go on loving you, I won't be able to stop myself.

Instead she went to the window and stared sightlessly out. 'Only for your father's sake,' she said again. After a few minutes she turned. 'But at least let's turn on the television. I can't stand sitting here with you, enduring your presence without something to take my mind off——' Off what? The power of your attraction, the magnetism about you that draws me, despite myself?

The television was switched on. It was a studio discussion and, after a while, Anona's mind drifted, thinking impossible thoughts about the man seated only a few feet away. It was only when she was conscious of being scooped into two strong arms that she realised she had been sleeping.

'Put me down,' she said indignantly, 'put me down at once!'

He ignored her plea, merely telling her to be quiet. At the door she asked, 'Where are we going?'

'I'm taking you home. Disappointed? Did you think we were on our way to my bedroom?'

'If you don't put me down, Shane Brodie,' she hissed in a loud whisper, 'I'll scream!'

Unceremoniously he let her body slide through his arms to stand on her own feet.

As the car braked in front of her father's cottage, she opened the door and got out. Momentarily she waited, but Shane did not speak. Unreasonably annoyed, she stalked along the garden path, hearing the car accelerate away. She had done him a favour by spending the evening with him, yet he had not even had the courtesy to say 'goodnight'.

It was towards the end of the following afternoon that Anona knocked on Shane's door and was invited by him to enter. He looked up but did not smile.

'What do you want to do about this evening?' she asked tonelessly.

He leant back in his chair and flicked a glance over her. 'Do you mean do I require your services?' With a mocking smile he regarded her quick flush of anger. 'The answer's no, thanks all the same. Even my father wouldn't expect our passion to continue unabated and without rest at such heights.'

Infuriated by his cynical smile, she replied, 'I won't ask again. Next time you'll have to do the asking.'

'Oh, I will,' was his sarcastic answer. 'I'll beg you on my knees to give me the pleasure of your company.'

'Oh, go to——'

His loud laughter cut off the last word.

May Howton stayed on that evening even though she knew Anona would not be going out with Shane. Anona had observed recently how close May and her father were growing. When May, helping with the evening meal, mentioned that Will had asked if, after his daughter had married, she would be prepared to live in the cottage with him, Anona showed no surprise.

'As his housekeeper, I suppose,' she commented.

'As his wife,' May corrected her. When, after a pause, Anona smiled and hugged her, May sighed with relief.

Anona said, 'Did you really think I'd disapprove of you as a stepmother? I'm delighted at the prospect.'

'Your father asked me if I would tell you,' May explained. 'He said that I had the gentle touch which he lacked and would break the news to you more tactfully.'

Anona smiled. 'I must go and tell him how pleased I am.' May nodded understandingly and went on with her work.

Anona's arms went round her father's frail figure. 'Did you think I was still a child and would resent your bringing a fearsome "mother-figure" into our home?' she teased.

Will smiled. 'Perhaps I did. I still can't adjust completely to the fact that you're no longer a small girl. However much I keep telling myself, "Anona's an engaged woman. She'll soon be married," it doesn't seem to register on my subconscious mind.'

If only she could blurt out, Oh, but I'm not really engaged at all. It's only for your friend Morris's sake that Shane and I are pretending. But telling him the truth was impossible because then she would have to tell her father why, and that would mean the end of his friendship with Morris.

She would also have to leave Brodie's and she would never see Shane again.

Next morning she was on the telephone at the office, taking details from a customer about a load he wanted taken up-country, when Shane walked in.

He waited until she had finished, then, making sure she was alone, he said, 'I've got a prior engagement tonight.'

'Which means I'm free again.'

Spencer chose that moment to enter. 'Free, is she?' he joked. 'This is my chance. Anona, will you come out with me?'

Shane said coldly to his cousin, 'Since when has it been your habit to poach on other people's property?'

'Whew! You really have staked your claim, mate.'

Anona flushed and had opened her mouth to protest when Shane said, 'You chose unfortunate words, Spencer.'

'Sorry, Anona,' said Spencer, 'but your fiancé referring to you as his property led me to believe—well, you know.'

'It's okay,' Anona answered, with a half-smile. Only to

Shane did she let her flashing eyes show her anger. Which, she decided, was a stupid thing to do since getting angry with Shane was exposing a weakness he would surely play on when the time was right.

'If you meant it, Spencer,' she said defiantly, 'I'd like to go out with——'

He raised a hand. 'I wouldn't dare defy my cousin who is, after all, my boss.' He grinned at Shane. 'I like the money he pays me for working for him too much to lose it by taking out the girl he's going to marry.'

'But——' The word was out before she knew and Shane's eyes froze her protest in her throat.

'Tomorrow, *darling*,' Shane said, 'we can go to my place. My father will be out.'

When he had gone, Spencer looked covertly at Anona. 'His place, eh? You'll be alone, will you?'

'He's only pretending,' Anona commented offhandedly.

' "Pretending" you call it? I'd call it the real thing, in capital letters. No woman's ever got under his skin this way before, and has he had plenty!'

If only Spencer knew, Anona thought. He still hasn't allowed a woman to get 'under his skin', not even the girl to whom he had once proposed marriage. What if he hadn't been the one to cause her father's injuries and she hadn't returned his ring? Would he have remained faithful to her all his life, or would he have strayed, unable to resist those 'other women'?

CHAPTER ELEVEN

MAY went home at her usual time after helping Anona wash the dishes left over from the evening meal. As she walked down the garden path, pushing her bicycle, a car drew up at the curb and Morris Brodie emerged, the tall, solid, gangling length of him.

They talked for a moment at the gate, then Morris made his way to the front door where Anona stood waiting to welcome him. 'Is your father in the mood for a visitor?' Morris asked in his loud, carrying voice.

'Welcome in, Morris,' Will called. 'Been longing for a game of chess. I was hoping you'd come.'

Morris lowered himself into his usual chair and answered Anona's solicitous enquiry about his health. 'I'm fine now,' he said. 'I go up and down. Mostly up, though, thank goodness. And we're not getting any younger, are we, Will?'

'My father's an engaged man, did he tell you?' Anona announced.

'He's not!' Anona nodded. 'Who's the lucky lady, Will? May Howton?' Will said yes, and Morris burst out, 'Why, he's blushing, my old friend Will's gone red as a schoolboy!'

There was laughter and Morris leant across to shake Will's hand. 'Like daughter like father, to play about with an old saying,' said Morris.

Engaged! Anona fidgeted with the ring on her finger. No longer hers, only there to please—no, why wasn't she honest —to fool an ailing man.

'I'm going for a drive, Father,' she said, 'and maybe a walk.'

Will nodded indifferently. Now his old friend was there,

he did not need her. Soon, when May became his wife, he would not need his daughter at all. What then?

Morris said, 'Shane's gone out tonight. Don't know where. He wouldn't tell me.' He looked enquiringly at Anona, who shook her head.

'A prior engagement, he told me,' she answered.

Morris looked baffled, then lifted his bulky shoulders and gave his mind to the chess pieces which Will was setting out on the board.

Anona drove into Bakewell, parking the car and strolling round the quiet streets. She window-shopped, since the shops had closed some time earlier. She passed the great scrolled and figured Saxon cross and saw the Rutland Arms which was mentioned in Jane Austen's *Pride and Prejudice*.

The tale of the famous Bakewell Pudding had been told to her by her father. It had originated there and had happened as a result of a misunderstanding between the mistress of the hotel and her cook.

In the distance she saw the five Gothic arches of the bridge over the River Wye which was built around 1300 and was, she had been told, one of the oldest bridges in England.

The hills beyond called to her and she drove in their direction, regardless of the fact that the air was chilling as the sun descended. She reached the road below the summit of Mam Tor while the sun was still high enough not to force her to think twice about making for the summit of the mountain.

Having parked the car, she started walking. The climb was a little rough, but she had remembered to put on walking shoes. When she topped the summit, the view spreading below and far into the distance was of immense beauty and splendour. If Shane had been at her side as he had been before when they had come to this area, she could have asked little more of life.

Her mind left her eyes to scan the landscape of valleys and hills with its patchwork-like fields and scattered trees and thought about things nearer to her heart. A prior engagement, Shane had told everyone, so where had he gone? Engagement. Her fingers clenched and relaxed around the ring he had made her replace on her finger.

In the changing circumstances of her life, she could no longer continue to pretend that she was engaged to Shane. If the news were broken gently to Shane's father, she was sure he would come to accept it calmly as one of those things that happened in these days of changing relationships.

Having filled her lungs with fresh moorland air and her mind with their tranquillity, she hurried in the approaching darkness to her car and drove away from the hills and valleys towards her home.

A car was coming from the opposite direction and the road was narrow. It was necessary to slow down and let the larger car take the initiative. When it was only a few feet away she recognised the shape and the registration number. The shock of meeting Shane out here on the moors—yes, there was a girl beside him, and her name was Lidia, with the beautiful face and figure—made Anona's whole body shake.

The driver's eyes, as his car went slowly past, flicked up to meet Anona's. His held no surprise, only blankness. He must have recognised her smaller car as soon as he had seen it. He drove on without a flicker of recognition.

For a few moments Anona sat, unable to move. Inside she was shaking and like a piece of Mam Tor, the Shivering Mountain, she was sure she felt a vital part of her move and slip away into oblivion. She felt as if the very heart of her had gone for ever.

'I'm sorry, but the pretence is over.' Anona faced Shane across his desk. In the palm of her hand was his ring. 'If you explain to your father that we discovered we were just not made for each other, I'm certain he'll understand.'

Since Shane did not take the ring, she placed it on his

blotter. After a moment's thought he reached out, picked it up and pocketed it.

'I hope,' Anona said bitterly, 'that you enjoyed your evening with Miss Harmon-Park.' She persisted, against her better judgment, 'I'm glad I learnt before it was too late that even during a mock-engagement you couldn't keep your distance from other women.' A black eyebrow lifted, as if in query, but Shane said nothing. 'You did warn me that day you gave me a lift. No staying power but plenty of straying power.'

His face was a mask, his eyes as hard as the rocks on the hills. He did not speak but seemed to be waiting for her to leave. It was only when she reached the door that he said,

'Tomorrow I'm going away for a few days. To Newcastle for a conference, if you want to know.'

'I don't want to know. I don't want to know anything more about you. I can't even think why I agreed to play along with you about the so-called engagement.'

'It was for my father's sake, remember?'

'Yes, I remember.' She added, her voice high and thin, 'Your father's worth a hundred of you.'

Shane gave a brief, sarcastic bow.

She could not return at once to her room, she decided, making instead for the ladies' room. There she sat on a chair and held her head, hoping no one else would come in. She couldn't allow herself the release of crying because the aftermath of the tears would show.

It was not until she arrived home and had run, greeting no one, up to her room, that she gave way to her shattered emotions. Later, after tidying her hair and using a little make-up in a vain attempt to cover her tear-marks, she went down to meet the inevitable questions.

May was in the kitchen, preparing the meal. There was a question in her eyes as she saw Anona's ravaged face. In answer, Anona held out her empty left hand.

'Do you want to talk about it?'

'Later, May, perhaps,' she answered. 'I'll have to tell Father. When——?'

'The sooner the better,' May advised, and Anona nodded.

In the living-room, her father was making notes, textbooks spread around him. 'Father,' said Anona, and he looked up. She held out her hand, showing him. 'The engagement's over.'

A frown creased his brows. 'Oh. May I ask why?'

'Would—would incompatibility answer your question?'

Will sighed. 'It will suffice, I suppose.' He saw the tearmarks. 'You're upset. Whose idea was it to end the engagement?'

She moistened her lips. 'Let's say it was—mutual.'

Should she tell him the real reason? No, that she could never do. It would mean that he would feel it was wrong to go on seeing his good friend Morris Brodie, and she would never be responsible for depriving him of that pleasure.

Will frowned again. 'Strange how I always seemed to know his face, even from the first meeting.'

Anona panicked. If he started to delve, of how much would his good memory remind him? 'Your—your visits to Shane's college? You said so yourself, didn't you?'

'Could be. Somehow I never did take to the man. I tried to like him for your sake, but there was always—something, some obstacle that stopped me.'

Anona could only hope that the 'obstacle' to which he referred would never be broken through and that nothing would take him back to those terrible moments just after the accident had happened. In her mind she was certain that that was where he had first seen Shane.

It was later, while her father was going through his notes with May, that the telephone rang. Shane? Anona thought, but immediately quelled her hopes. It was over between them. Couldn't she get herself to understand?

'Anona? Morris Brodie here. My dear, Shane's told me.

But why, dear, why? You looked so in love.' He seemed agitated and Anona grew alarmed. Had Shane been right? Should they have kept up the pretence of the engagement for longer than they had? But for how long? Morris's trouble would never go away.

'Didn't Shane tell you, Mr Brodie? We—we just found we weren't well, compatible. You know, our tastes were so different, our outlook on—on life, our——' How long could she go on lying? 'Well, everything.'

'But Anona, love would overcome all that. Given time, you'd grow together, agree to differ and laugh at those differences. Surely you must know that?'

It was like twisting a knife in your own heart, Anona thought. 'It just wouldn't have worked, Mr Brodie. So we decided to finish it before we—before too much—much damage had been done.'

'Anona,' his voice was heavy, 'was that truly all? Was there anything else that caused you to part?'

He was surely thinking of the accident, of Shane's part in it! Quickly she reassured him, as best she could, on that point, although without actually mentioning it. She did not want her father to overhear. Morris seemed in the end to be convinced and when he rang off, she felt as cold and shivering as if she had been wandering for hours in a driving blizzard.

As she walked along the corridor to her office next morning, Shane came out of his. He seemed ready to leave. A briefcase was in his hand, his suit of the finest quality, his broad shoulders appearing even broader through the excellent cut of the jacket. Tentatively she smiled, only to receive in return a cold, repelling look.

Well, she should have expected it. Hadn't she told him she didn't want to know *anything* about him any more? He had taken the bold, defiant statement at its face value.

It was two hours later that the crisis arose. Spencer was away for the day. He had left at eight o'clock, having taken an empty truck to Manchester to be loaded for delivery in

London. There had been no one else available to go at such short notice. Anona had been left in charge and she felt that things were under control.

One of the drivers was expected back within the hour and he was due to take a trailer loaded with machinery to Dover. As the time passed with no sign of him, some sixth sense told Anona that something had gone wrong. The load for Dover simply had to be on its way on time.

When the phone rang, she pounced on it. 'Brodie's Transport,' she said. 'Anona Willis speaking.'

'Sam here, Miss Willis. I've got bad news—my truck's broken down. It's in a layby. I thumbed a lift in a car and I've rung a garage. They're sending someone out to the truck, but it could be hours before I'm on my way again.'

'But Sam,' she wailed, 'that load for Dover. It's got to catch the ferry to Dunkirk.'

'Don't I know it!' said Sam. 'It's been worrying me sick while I've been hanging around. The trailer's got a full load of machinery and it's due in Paris tomorrow morning.'

'It says here,' Anona consulted a letter on the file, 'that there'll be some important foreign buyers waiting to receive the goods.'

'Look, miss, is Mr Spencer Brodie there? No? Well, Mr Shane Brodie, then. Not him, either? Miss Willis, have you got a headache on your hands!'

'Oh, Sam, if only Mr Rob could drive a truck! What shall I do, Sam?'

'No other drivers available, miss? No, there wouldn't be. I checked just in case something like this happened. But I counted on Mr Spencer Brodie being free. Short of jumping in the cab and driving the truck yourself, Miss Willis,' Sam tried to joke, 'I just can't think of anything.'

'Well, it's my worry, Sam, not yours. You've got enough. I'll find someone.'

'That load's got to go, miss,' Sam advised just before ringing off.

Did she dare? Anona wondered, tapping agitatedly on

the desk. Did she dare call Morris Brodie? Maybe he'd know someone——?

'Emergency, dear?' said Morris, a comforting voice at the other end of the line. 'That Dover load? Yes, I know about it. Shane keeps me up to date. Yes, I know it's important.'

'It says here, Mr Brodie, that a high rate's been charged just because it's so important. At a time like this, could Brodie's ask another transport company to help out? Like lending one of their drivers?'

'You won't get help at this short notice,' Morris told her. 'Not in the summer when people go off for the summer holiday, truck drivers included. Give me ten minutes, Anona. I'll come up with something.'

As the minutes passed and there was no call back, Anona started to fret and then to grow thoroughly alarmed. Her hand was hovering over the telephone when she heard Morris Brodie's booming voice along the corridor.

Her door came open and he was there, dressed in a Brodie's overall and cap, a food bag and flask in his hand and a look of eager anticipation on his face. Despite his age and his ailment, he was still a fine figure of a man, full of vigour and an appetite for life and living.

'I'm ready, my dear. Where's that truck?'

'You, Mr Brodie? But you can't, you can't!'

'Oh?' He tried to put on a proprietorial air, but a·grin wiped away the autocratic look. 'Who says I can't? The girl my son's going to marry?'

'He's——' She stopped. He'd forgotten, in his excitement he still thought they were in love! Never mind, let him think that way. At this precise moment in time, nothing mattered except that she must at all costs stop Morris Brodie from carrying out his crazy scheme.

'I won't let you go, Mr Brodie. I'd never forgive myself if—if something went wrong.'

'Like what?' said Morris Brodie, on his dignity.

'Like——' She had to be tactful. 'Like the truck breaking down, like Sam's truck has.'

'That wasn't a Brodie's truck he was driving, it was a hired one. A Brodie's truck doesn't break down. Now come on, young woman, we're wasting valuable time. I want to be on my way. Find all those papers I need.'

While Anona, her face scarlet with anxiety and pressure, went through the appropriate folder, Morris stood at the window, staring at the passing traffic.

'I've been waiting for this moment,' he said. 'It's been my dream, taking out a truck again. Climbing in, being in charge. D'you know, when I've seen a truck go out sometimes, part of me has gone with it. I never mind being alone in the driving cab. A truck driver never must mind. He's got his freedoms, but he's got his responsibilities, too. He's got to see his load gets there, wherever that is, come what may. And that's what I'm going to do.'

He turned from the window. 'Brodie's have got a reputation for reliability, and I'm seeing they keep it. Got the papers yet, dear?' His face was flushed, he was as excited as a small boy going to his first party.

The papers were in Anona's hands, but she held on to them. 'Mr Brodie, I ask you once more, please don't——'

He wasn't listening. 'Come on. I want the consignee's copy and the receipt note. I get a signature on that for the delivery of the goods. You put the file copy back in the file. All right, dear?'

Numbed with worry at what she was allowing Shane's father to do, Anona nodded.

'Right,' said Morris, 'here we go.'

Anona went with him, down the stairs, in the Brodie's van driven by Jim to the filling station and the depot at the back where the trucks, both empty and loaded, were garaged.

Anona got quickly out of the van and ran across to the shop to see if Rob was there, but Albert, the man employed part-time to take customers' money, said that Mr Rob had taken the day off and had driven to London. Disappointed, Anona hurried out. She had hoped, as a last resort, that Rob would persuade his father to change his mind.

Round the back, Morris was climbing into the truck. 'Shall I come with you, Mr Brodie?' she asked, gazing up at him as he settled into the driver's seat.

'No, lass, no. What would I do with a lass like you to distract me by talking?'

'I'll keep as quiet as a mouse, Mr Brodie.'

He laughed. 'You go back and look after that office. I'm fine. It's wonderful up here. I'm back where I belong, in charge of a truck.'

'What will your doctor say?' she asked desperately.

'I don't care a damn for doctors. Didn't I tell you? You die if you see them, you die if you don't. That's my motto!' He started up the engine and Jim murmured that she went like a bird.

Giving a thumbs-up sign, Morris Brodie drove the truck out of the yard slowly and carefully, and on to the road. 'See you in the morning!' he roared over the engine revs, and then he was among the traffic and a giant, receding blob of red backed with green canvas covering, diminishing to nothing in the distance.

'Oh, Jim,' Anona's hands covered her face. 'What shall I do? What will Mr Shane say?'

'Don't take on, Miss Willis. Mr Morris'll be all right, you see. He's tough, that man. He came up the hard way. He'll make it.'

Spencer turned pale when he heard the news that evening on his return.

'Uncle Morris taken that load to Dover? Anona, how could you have *let* him? Don't you know the state of his health?'

'Spencer, I couldn't stop him, honestly I couldn't. I *had*

to contact him, there was no one else. I thought he might know of another transport firm that would help us out.'

'Another firm, when it's Brodie's load? Can you imagine Morris Brodie letting someone else do our work for us?' He sighed heavily. 'You weren't to know that, I guess.' He ran a distracted hand over his red hair. 'We'll just have to hope——'

The telephone rang in Anona's room. She raced through and seized the receiver. Her hand was trembling.

'Anona, love? Morris here.' He sounded jubilant. 'I made it, Anona. I told you I would. I'm starting back now with the empty truck.'

'But Mr Brodie, couldn't you stay in London, sleep in a bed in a comfortable hotel? Surely there's no need to come back straight away?'

'I'm doing it properly, dear. I'm sleeping on the bunk bed in this truck. It's comfortable, got all a man needs overnight. I'll get a bite to eat, then I'll be on my way. By heaven, Anona love, have I enjoyed myself! It's been like a dream come true. You tell that fiancé of yours, that arrogant son of mine, I managed it after all.'

'Mr Brodie, here's Spencer.' She passed the receiver to Spencer.

'Uncle? Yes, I heard everything. You talk loud on the phone.' There was laughter. 'Yes, of course I congratulate you, but you take care on the way back.'

As he rang off, Spencer shook his head. 'Nearly two years since he drove a truck, and he had to choose one that was loaded with machinery! But he's managed it, so now we can relax a bit.'

'He's got the return journey to make,' Anona reminded him.

'With an empty truck there should be no strain, nothing like a loaded one. He should arrive here probably early afternoon, depending of course on what time he starts his journey.'

'Do you know where Shane's staying?' She remembered the last time she hadn't known the name of his hotel. Rob had told her—grudgingly.

Spencer looked at her, surprised. 'Yes. Don't you?'

Anona found herself hiding her bare engagement finger. 'He went off in such a hurry I forgot to ask.' She went on swiftly, 'Should we contact him, tell him about his father?'

'Before Uncle Morris phoned, I'd have said yes, but now we know he's okay, I doubt if it's necessary.'

It was later, as she was preparing for bed, that Anona was caught by an odd feeling of apprehension. She wished she hadn't listened to Spencer, but had asked him for Shane's hotel number. A thought kept spinning in her head—Shane should be told, he should be told . . .

Before breakfast she called Spencer at his home. Surprised, but without asking questions, he gave her the hotel number, probably assuming, Anona supposed, that she just wanted to hear her loving fiancé's voice.

It was her ex-fiancé's voice she heard, but it could hardly be described as loving. 'Brodie here,' he said, his tone clipped.

'You sound,' it slipped out without thinking, 'as though you've got out of bed on the wrong side.'

There was a pause, an impatient sigh, then nothing.

Reproaching herself for stepping over the line—he was, after all, no longer connected with her in any emotional way —she said, 'Anona Willis speaking.'

'So I gathered. Well?'

Her heart, which had quickened at the sound of his voice, now began to thump painfully. It was hardly good news that she had to impart. 'Have you had your breakfast?'

'Just. Why? Why the hell should you want to know that?'

Thank goodness he's eaten, she thought. He'd need all his strength. 'Shane, I——' She bit her lip, mauled it, stopped when she felt the soreness, then went on, finding a scraping of courage, 'I let your father take a truck out.'

He said, after a few moments in which he might have counted to ten, 'No, I can't have heard you correctly. Tell me again, slowly, so my early morning brain can take it in.'

'I let your father take a truck out.'

It was as though he was holding his breath.

'Sam got held up,' she plunged on. 'He called me and told me his truck had broken down. It would hold him up for hours. And there was that load. It had to go—it was urgent.'

'Not——' There seemed to be a catch in his voice. 'Not that load of machinery for Dunkirk via Dover?'

'That one, Shane. You see,' she rushed on, 'Spencer was away with a truck in Manchester and there was no spare driver around. I didn't know what to do so I phoned your father. Honestly, Shane, I didn't think I was doing wrong in asking his advice. I thought he'd know of another transport firm.'

'My father give away a Brodie contract? Are you mad? Don't you know about that reputation for reliability that's the life-blood of a family firm like ours? Don't you know that the members of that family would go to almost *any* lengths to carry out a contract?'

The tears that were trickling down her cheeks showed up in her voice. 'No, I didn't, Shane. Not to that extent, anyway. I didn't dream he'd turn up here all dressed and ready to drive the truck himself. He seemed so happy about it, Shane, so confident.'

'My God, girl, don't you know the state of his heart?'

'Shane,' she swallowed her tears and smiled, 'he managed it. He called us last night. He'd arrived safely and was starting back empty. He'd sleep in the truck, he said. He was so *happy*, Shane,' she repeated lamely.

There was a short, thinking pause. 'I'm quitting the conference here and coming back.'

'Shane, no! There's no need. Spencer said that with an empty truck the going would be easy.'

'I'm coming back.' The receiver's slam hurt her ear.

May arrived early, as Anona came off the phone. She saw the tears, asked why they were there. Anona shook her head and put a finger to her lips. She did not want her father, who was still sleeping in his downstairs room, to know about his friend Morris's exploits until the man had returned to base, safe and well. May just patted her shoulder and seemed to assume that it was the broken engagement that had upset her.

It was half-past midday when Shane's car screeched to a halt outside the main office building and his steps, taking the stairs two at a time, raced inexorably upward. He flung open Spencer's door and asked. 'Is he back yet?'

Anona rushed in. 'He shouldn't be long, Shane. He'd have made an early start, wouldn't he, sleeping in the truck. Any—any minute, I should think.'

His icy eyes made her freeze up inside. 'Would you keep out of this?'

'Why?' Her anxiety had been eating into her, but she had all the time pacified herself with reassurances, although they had had precious little foundation. Now her control snapped. 'Why should I? Is it because I'm not one of the family? Never will be now?' Spencer stared at her, saw her empty left hand and his eyes opened wider.

Hands on hips, Shane came towards her. 'Why? Because *you* were the bloody fool who let him go, that's why. You should have done something, *anything*, to stop him!'

'Such as punctured the tires? What about that reputation for reliability you all put at the top of your lists? Should I have run off with his shoes or asked doctors to put him in a strait-jacket? *That* would have been the only way you'd have stopped your father!'

'What about Rob?'

'I was told he'd refused to learn to drive a truck.'

'He refused—at first. I made him learn. He passed, but he hasn't taken out a truck since he passed his test.'

'She wasn't to know that, Shane,' Spencer intervened, trying to rationalise the argument.

'In any case,' said Anona, 'Rob had taken the day off and gone to London.'

'There were plenty of other people who would have helped in some way. Elsa, Rob's wife, she's got contacts. Why didn't you ask her?'

Anona was silent.

'Go on,' Spencer urged, 'tell him. Elsa had gone off for the day with her husband.'

Shane's lips thinned. 'I'm going to the depot to wait for my father.' Anona ran after him, calling, 'I'm coming, too.'

As he parked near the repair shop, there was the roar of a truck. Anona, following Shane, raced to the courtyard.

'He's back!' Anona gasped. Still following, she ran round to the driver's door.

'I did it, son, I did it!' Morris shouted, hands lifted high in a victory clasp above his head. Then, with the door half open, he pressed his fist to his chest. 'That pain again, darn it. It's the third time ... Oh, God, son ...'

Shane was climbing up, shouting for help. Rob came rushing out. 'Get his legs,' Shane snapped, and eased his father's limp figure from the driving cab. Rob lowered his father's legs gently and they put him full-length on the ground. Shane tore off his jacket and made it into a pillow for his father's head. Morris's face was ashen, the colour almost gone from his lips.

'A doctor,' Shane told his brother, 'an ambulance, anything!' Rob rushed off.

Morris's eyes flickered open and he started to speak, so quietly they strained to hear him. 'Too late, son. Just listen, will you?' He paused for a dragging breath. 'I enjoyed it, every minute. I knew I was taking a risk, but it had been a dream, you see, a constant dream since—since——' His eyes closed, opened again. Another gasping breath. 'Anona,' she was there bending over him, 'say "hallo" to Will for me. Tell him he was the best friend I ever had.'

The tears ran down Anona's face as she nodded.

'Shane—son—tell her the truth.' His voice was barely a

whisper. 'I know why you broke up. I'm not stupid. Tell her the truth ...' His head flopped sideways on to Shane's shoulder as Rob came rushing out again. Morris's hand lifted towards his younger son, then dropped lifelessly.

Three weeks later, Shane called Anona into his office. She had not seen him since the day his father had died. Spencer and Elsa had shared Shane's work between them.

'He's got problems,' said Spencer, 'dealing with his father's estate. The will Uncle Morris left was by no means straightforward. And Shane's gone away visiting Brodie's various provincial offices. He's taken over completely now,' Spencer had added. 'He offered Rob a partnership, but Rob wasn't interested.'

Now Anona faced Shane across his desk. His eyes were shadowed, and he looked tired and drawn. 'Please sit down,' he invited.

It was, Anona thought, occupying a low chair, as though she was a visitor, a stranger, as though he had never held her in his arms, kissing her with a passion that touched her deepest fires to life.

She sat because her legs felt weak and because she, too, was tired, weary with a loving unreturned, with waiting— but for what? She, too, had suffered after Morris had died, feeling deeply the loss of the big, happy man, standing by and watching her father mourn, unable to pacify him.

There was also, among her sadness, a sense of having been indirectly responsible for Morris's death, although her reason told her, in retrospect, that at the time she had been powerless to change the course which events had taken.

Shane walked about with a restlessness that appeared to have been his way of life in the past three weeks. He had never before, to her knowledge, behaved in this 'caged tiger' fashion.

'How did your father take my father's death?' he asked at last, pausing in front of her and looking down at her set features.

'Badly, very badly.' Her father had, she recalled, stared at her white-faced. Then, when she had passed on Morris's last message, he held his face in his hands. His tears, which he had tried to hide, had come seeping through his fingers.

When she had bent down, trying to comfort him, he had shaken her off and she had left him to mourn alone. After a while, May had said, 'I'll go in. I'll do what I can to soothe him. You don't mind, dear?'

May, as his future wife, had succeeded where Anona, his daughter, had failed.

Haltingly, Anona tried to convey all this to Shane, who listened without comment or change of expression.

At last he said, 'This evening, are you free?' Anona nodded. 'Would you come to my house? There's something I have to say to you.'

She knew at once what that 'something' was. He would ask her to resign from her job at Brodie's. He'd be kind, of course, and offer to keep her on until she had found some other occupation, promising to give her excellent references. He would not tell her the truth—that he still held her responsible for his father's death.

'Can't you say it here?' she asked, her eyes challenging.

'Sorry,' his manner was autocratic, 'it's impossible. Will you come?' He appeared to be growing irritated. She nodded and he said dismissively, 'Seven-thirty.' With that she had to be content.

Anona told May where she was going, but she let her father believe she intended to drive into the hills.

'Another evening drive?' he commented irritably. 'Are you still lamenting the breaking off of your engagement? You weren't like this the last time.'

The last time! Yes, she sighed inwardly, she was becoming expert in the art of backing out of promises to marry, breaking up relationships which threatened to tie her down. Or that was probably how it appeared to an onlooker.

Shane himself opened the door. Of course, there was no one else now, no big, welcoming man to extend his hand

and his warmth and to tell her to make herself at home. Under Shane's withdrawn, utterly serious gaze, she certainly did not feel at home.

He took her into the living-room and she sat uncomfortably on the couch. Morris's presence seemed to linger on, tauntingly, uncannily. It seemed in Anona's imagination to dog Shane's restless footsteps, and to sit invisibly beside her. She could even sense a feeling of disquiet in the air—emanating from herself, probably.

Her choice of clothing had been a simple sleeveless dress in blue and white, with a low-pointed neckline trimmed with a white collar. Her sandals were white, matching her handbag. It was as though she were going for an interview. Well, she had been right, hadn't she? There was only formality between them now, no touching, no laughter, no intertwining limbs and breathless kisses.

'Thank you for coming,' Shane said politely.

'It's my pleasure,' she answered, equally politely, but she caught him eyeing her narrowly for sarcasm. If only she could tell him how sincerely she had meant it!

He sat at last, throwing himself into the chair his father used to occupy. 'Those last words my father spoke—you heard them?' She nodded, but he repeated them. *'Tell her the truth.'* There was a long pause. He said at last, his eyes closed, his head against the chair back, 'It goes very much against the grain, but I have to carry out his last wish.' He was silent for so long, she said in a small voice,

'What truth, Shane?'

'The truth about the accident, when one of our trucks knocked your father down.'

Anona found that she was holding her breath.

'I've told no one else,' he went on, 'not one member of the family. But I have to tell you, because my father wished it.' His eyes opened, turned to rest on her expectant, vital young face, then closed again. He went on,

'My father had had a heart attack, a bad one. It took him two or three months to recover. He became restless and said if he didn't drive a truck soon, he'd lose his touch, forget how—you know how it is.'

His eyes opened again and slewed round towards her to catch her nod. He went on, staring unseeingly into the garden through the french windows, 'I argued that he was not in a fit state to drive a truck, probably never would be again. I tried to persuade him to get his doctor's advice first. Then he said if I didn't come out with him, he'd go alone.'

There was a short pause, as if the memory he was experiencing was painful. 'At first I drove,' he continued, 'finding a quiet road where he could take over. He drove slowly at first, then faster, finding his way, against my wishes, to the main road and turning back to the town.

'My father stopped the truck quite correctly at a crossing, allowing people across the road. A man was walking along, but suddenly changed direction and stepped on to the road just as the truck was gathering speed.'

He went on quickly now, as if wanting to bring the relating of the incident to an end. 'It happened a short distance ahead of the crossing. Luckily my father, being cautious, had not pressed his foot too heavily on the accelerator. If he had, there would have been more serious consequences. The truck hit the man——'

'My father?' Anona broke in, her voice a whisper.

'Your father. He was sent flying by the impact, seriously injured, but still alive. My father went so white I was afraid for him. I thought he might have another heart attack and decided on the spot to take the blame. I pushed him down, somehow manoeuvred him across to my seat while I moved over to the driving seat. I told him to stay where he was and not to get out under any circumstances.'

'So you went to my father——?'

He nodded. 'Others were there first, but I pushed them aside. I bent over him, lifting up his head. He was partly conscious and his eyes opened and closed.'

'Which is why he's sworn from the moment you both met that he'd seen you before?'

Shane nodded. 'He said, and all the others—about a dozen people—heard him say it, "It was my fault, my fault. I was thinking about my work." Then he lost consciousness. You know the rest.'

Anona frowned. 'There was a newspaper report, a small one. I don't remember your name being mentioned.'

'A Brodie driver, was all they were told when they called us by phone for a statement. We refused to give the driver's name. The whole matter was passed to our insurance company.'

'I know. And they,' Anona filled in, 'dealt with the matter through my father's solicitors.'

'Your father again admitted liability, so there was no case.'

'You didn't even offer an *ex gratia* payment,' she complained with bitterness.

'We did, against our insurance company's advice. Your father refused it.'

'Are you sure? He didn't tell me.'

'Did he show you every piece of correspondence?'

Anona could only shake her head. Her father was sometimes secretive about his private affairs, even about the Brodie accident. 'I'm sorry,' she said at last. 'So,' she moistened her lips, 'it means that not only are you completely innocent, but—but a kind of hero, into the bargain.'

His eyes did not waver from hers and he stayed completely still.

'You were a wonderful son to your father.' Why did her voice have to falter? 'You protected him by taking the blame for something he did.'

Still Shane was silent. He stood then, thrusting his hands into his pockets and walking to gaze out into the garden which was a riot of colour with summer flowers.

'He only agreed to the deception,' Shane said at last, 'for

the sake of the company. He never ceased to reproach himself for hiding behind me.'

Anona said, her voice low and choked, 'Why did you let me go on accusing you, calling you names, even breaking off our engagement? Unless—unless that was what you wanted?'

His back remained rigid. Its indifference goaded her to an irrational fury. She ran across the distance between them, but he did not turn.

'You deceived me,' she cried, waiting for him to look at her. He stayed with his back towards her. 'You—you cheat, you hypocrite!' She was hammering on his back now, short, hard blows with the palms of her hands. 'Why did you propose to me? Was it guilty conscience, a way you thought out of making up to my father for all he'd lost?'

He swung round, catching her wrists in a cruel grip. '*Who* proposed? I seem to remember that it was you, in a roundabout way. You told Rob, didn't you, boasting that you were the girl who'd "caught" me, whereas all the others had failed.'

'You did ask me to marry you after that, you *did*!' The memory of that moment flashed before her eyes. It was like a sudden burst of sunshine, blinding her, making her eyes water. 'So it could still mean you did it just to satisfy your guilty conscience——'

'Why guilty?' he asked quietly, 'when I told you I had done nothing?'

He had deflated her with words, making her go limp. His hands released her wrists and they felt bruised and sore. She had been thinking in the old way, unable to rid herself of the secret condemnation of him for her father's injuries. Something must put things right in her mind, something must happen to wipe out the bad thoughts she had held, quite unjustly, about him, replacing them with the clean air of truth.

That 'something' must come from her. He had acted the

hero, with his bravery and courage in taking the blame from his father's frail shoulders. Her eyes lifted to the man she loved, loved, if anything, even more now than ever before. He looked unreadably back at her.

'Shane?' She swallowed back the tears which threatened. 'Before I go, I just want to let you know how—how much I love you. It happened, I think, the moment we met.' Her face was pale with tension. Her shoulders lifted and fell heavily. 'All right, so you don't want to marry me. It's Lidia you like, even love maybe, better than you ever loved me. I accept that. But I had to tell you. Thanks for—everything.'

She turned to the door, but he was there behind her, swinging her round and into his arms. He was kissing her with a passion that surpassed all the other times he had kissed her, over and over until she had to plead for mercy.

'Oh, my love,' he murmured, 'did you really think I'd let you walk out of my life? Do you think I'll *ever* let you go? From the moment I saw you—even *before* we met—I fell in love with you. I saw the back of your head, and I followed you for mile after mile.'

'Don't I know it,' she said, smiling up at him. 'I kept seeing your truck in my driving mirror and I wanted to say some rude words at it.'

He threw back his head, laughing, looking years younger, as if the troubles of the recent past had fallen away. Anona laughed with him. At that moment she could have sworn that something, somewhere, sighed and rested peacefully. Probably all her past anguish and pain, she reflected . . .

'Promise me something,' said Shane. 'Your father must never know that the man who became one of his best friends was the man who injured him so badly.'

She shook her head. 'I *must* tell him, Shane. When we're married, I want him to love you as a son——'

His hand went over her mouth. 'Let me take the blame. He'll adjust in time. Nothing must spoil his good memories of my father.'

For a long time she clung to him, wondering at the sacrifice the man she loved was proposing to make where his reputation was concerned. And all to protect her own father from disillusionment.

'It's no good, Shane,' she looked up at him, 'one day when the time is right, I must tell him. I must clear your name in his eyes and let him know what a wonderful son-in-law he has.'

'You know something, Miss Willis?' Shane said against her ear. Her bright eyes lifted to his. 'You're marrying me quickly, before you can make your escape again.'

She twisted from him, calling, 'Catch me if you can!'

He caught her at the door, swung her into his arms and carried her to the couch. He pushed her back among the cushions, kissing her with a deep, ruthless possession. Lifting his head, he said, 'What's Brodie's stays Brodie's.'

'The family motto. Your father told us once.'

'So take warning. Soon, very soon, you'll be mine. Your bright, laughing eyes, your impudent nose, your irresistible mouth—all mine.'

'How soon?' she whispered, tracing the hard ridge of his jaw.

Their eyes met and held and he moved slowly down towards her. 'Now, my love, would hardly be soon enough. You're so much a part of me, my thoughts, my life, my very self, I can't live without you. Does that answer your question?'

'Yes, oh yes!' was her breathless reply.

His arms around her tightened and they were lost in a world of their own.

Harlequin Presents...

The books that let you escape into the wonderful world of romance! Trips to exotic places...interesting plots...meeting memorable people... the excitement of love.... These are integral parts of Harlequin Presents— the heartwarming novels read by women everywhere.

Many early issues are now available. Choose from this great selection!

Choose from this list of Harlequin Presents editions

Relive a great romance...
Harlequin Presents 1980
Complete and mail this coupon today!

Harlequin Reader Service

In U.S.A.
MPO Box 707
Niagara Falls, N.Y. 14302

In Canada
649 Ontario St.
Stratford, Ontario, N5A 6W2

Please send me the following Harlequin Presents novels. I am enclosing my check or money order for $1.50 for each novel ordered, plus 59¢ to cover postage and handling.

☐ 165	☐ 175	☐ 184
☐ 166	☐ 176	☐ 185
☐ 168	☐ 177	☐ 186
☐ 169	☐ 178	☐ 187
☐ 170	☐ 179	☐ 188
☐ 172	☐ 181	☐ 189
☐ 173	☐ 182	☐ 190
☐ 174	☐ 183	☐ 191

Number of novels checked @ $1.50 each = $_____

N.Y. State residents add appropriate sales tax $_____

Postage and handling $_____ .59

TOTAL $_____

I enclose _____
(Please send check or money order. We cannot be responsible for cash sent through the mail.)

NAME _____
(Please Print)

ADDRESS _____

CITY _____

STATE/PROV. _____

ZIP/POSTAL CODE _____

Offer expires June 30, 1980.

00456406000